BRIDE PROTECTOR SEAL

BROTHERHOOD PROTECTORS SERIES BOOK #2

ELLE JAMES

TWISTED PAGE INC

BRIDE PROTECTOR SEAL

BROTHERHOOD PROTECTORS SERIES
BOOK #2

New York Times & *USA Today*
Bestselling Author

ELLE JAMES

EBOOK ISBN: 978-1-62695-036-8

ISBN PRINT: 978-1-62695-037-5

This story is dedicated to military men and women who separate from active duty and find it hard to fit in with the so-called real world. You are loved and appreciated for all you have done to protect this great nation!

Elle James

AUTHOR'S NOTE

Enjoy other military books by Elle James

Brotherhood Protector Series
Montana SEAL (#1)
Bride Protector SEAL (#2)
Montana D-Force (#3)
Cowboy D-Force (#4)
Montana Ranger (#5)
Montana Dog Soldier (#6)
Montana SEAL Daddy (#7)
Montana Ranger's Wedding Vow (#8)
Montana Rescue
Take No Prisoners Series
SEAL's Honor (#1)
SEAL's Ultimate Challenge (#1.5)
SEAL'S Desire (#2)
SEAL's Embrace (#3)
SEAL's Obsession (#4)
SEAL's Proposal (#5)
SEAL's Seduction (#6)
SEAL'S Defiance (#7)
SEAL's Deception (#8)
SEAL's Deliverance (#9)

Visit ellejames.com for more titles and release dates

For hot cowboys, visit her alter ego Myla Jackson at
mylajackson.com
and join Elle James and Myla Jackson's Newsletter at
http://ellejames.com/ElleContact.htm

CHAPTER 1

Axel Svenson, or Swede, as he preferred to be called, flexed his hand before he stuck it out. He found the scars were less disconcerting than proffering his left hand to shake. "Nice to meet you, ma'am."

"You can call me Allie. Ma'am makes me sound old." Alyssa Patterson took the hand without flinching. "No offense, but I can't say that I'm as thrilled to meet you. I really don't need a bodyguard, despite what my brother says."

"Yes, you do," her brother, Hank 'Montana' Patterson, said.

His first day on the job with the Brotherhood Protectors and Swede's first client didn't want his services. It wasn't exactly the way he'd pictured his initial assignment. From the way Montana had described the work, he'd expected to be allocated to a helpless rich person who needed someone to chauffeur, him or her, around. All he'd have to do was look big and

1

tough. With the scar on the side of his face, he had no doubt he could intimidate the hell out of most people.

Instead of a rich socialite, Montana had tasked Swede with protecting his kid sister. And she wasn't thrilled with the idea.

"If your sister doesn't want a bodyguard, why force one on her?" Swede asked.

Allie's eyes narrowed. "Wait, you're taking my side?"

Swede shrugged. "You're a grown-ass woman. If you don't think you need a bodyguard, you shouldn't have to accept one."

Allie turned to her brother and flashed a smile. "I might like this guy after all."

Sadie, Montana's wife, laughed.

Montana shot a brief frown at Allie and Sadie, and turned to Swede. "After several suspicious events, Allie's fiancé is concerned about her. And frankly, so am I."

"I have too much to do between now and the wedding to have someone on my heels slowing me down," Allie argued.

Montana gave her an "I'm the big brother" look. "You already agreed to Swede tagging along. Just shut up and let him."

Allie crossed her arms over her chest. "I'm going to a fitting, having my nails done and shopping for lingerie for the wedding night. That's when I'm not hauling hay, cleaning stalls and checking fences not only on the Bear Creek Ranch, but on the Double Diamond." She gave Swede a look that sized him up and found him lacking. "What do you know about any of those activities?"

He shrugged. "Nothing."

Allie rolled her eyes and turned back to Montana. "Let me guess, he's never been on a ranch, and doesn't know one end of a horse from another?"

Rather than allow himself to feel inadequate, Swede stiffened his back and straightened to his full six-feet-four inches. "I might not know my way around a ranch, but I'm good with a gun, I learn fast, I'm quick on my feet and highly observant."

She opened her mouth.

Swede pressed a finger to her lips. "Let me demonstrate." He gave her the same assessing stare she'd given him. "You came straight from the horse stalls you spoke of because you smell like manure, and you're tracking it into the house. You didn't take time to brush your hair this morning, likely because you had to clean the stalls and take care of the animals. Your hands are shaky, probably because you drink too much coffee. You haven't slept well in days, if the circles under your eyes are any indication. The lack of sleep has everything to do with all of the things you mentioned, plus you're worried your brother might be right and you might be in danger." He crossed his arms over his chest, much like she had. "Did I miss anything?"

"Great. And he's a smartass." Allie glared at her brother.

Montana raised his hands. "Hey, don't look at me. Take it up with your fiancé. He was the one who thought you needed protection. Maybe if you'd decided to marry one of the locals instead of a rich man who just bought a ranch in Montana because he could, you wouldn't be in any more danger than getting thrown by a horse."

"Do you hear yourself?" Allie asked. "You sound like our father."

Montana scowled and his jaw tightened.

His wife, Sadie, touched his arm. "Sweetheart, Allie has the right to choose her partner. Let her take up the bodyguard issue with Damien. He's the one who thinks she might need one. He can better explain his concerns."

Montana slipped an arm around Sadie's waist. "You're right." He turned to his sister. "I'm sorry. You can marry any rich jerk you want. I don't have to like it, and I'll tell you so, but if this is what you want, I won't stand in your way."

"Damn right, you won't." She lifted her head.

"At least let Swede tag along. If Damien is set on hiring a bodyguard, perhaps he can convince you." Montana held open his arms. "You know I love you, kid. I only want what's best for you."

Allie sucked in a deep breath, let it out and stepped into her brother's hug. "I guess that's your job."

"Yup. I wouldn't be a big brother unless I told you how I see it." Montana sniffed. "And Swede is right. You do smell like manure."

Allie punched him in the belly. "Thanks. Love you, too." She hugged her sister-in-law and patted her stomach. "Take care of my niece."

Sadie laid a hand over her flat abdomen. "I will." She hugged Allie. "Let Swede take care of you. I want our baby to know her Auntie Allie."

"I'll be around. I might be marrying a rich man who

travels all over the world, but my life is here in Montana."

"Don't forget..." Sadie touched her arm. "We have the final fitting for your dress the day after tomorrow."

Allie sighed. "I don't know why I had to have it altered. It fit just fine."

"The dress was too loose around your waist and too short," Sadie reminded her. "And no, you can't wear your favorite cowboy boots under it."

"Why?" Allie protested. "Nobody will see my feet."

"Because they'd smell like you do now. Like the inside of a horse stall." Montana turned her around. "Go on. Talk to Damien before you go back to the ranch."

Swede's chest tightened over the back-and-forth arguing between the siblings. Montana was lucky. He had a wife, a baby on the way, his sister and his father. For Swede, one of the hardest things about being processed out of the military was losing the only family he had. His SEAL team. The soldiers he'd met during his recovery had family members come visit them. Not Swede.

The whole recovery process would have been a lot harder but for two things: the Australian shepherd he'd rescued from the animal shelter, and the Delta-Force soldier he'd met during his physical therapy sessions. Bear Parker had been in the same boat as he was. No home to go to, no family to greet him when he got there. They'd gone out for a beer several times after therapy sessions. Which reminded Swede...

He hesitated before following Allie. "You know,

Montana, when you start getting more business, I know another man you might want to hire."

"Yeah?" Montana's brows rose. "Tell me."

"He's not a SEAL, but he's former Delta Force."

"I might have work for him. Is he available now? Or do we have to wait until his enlistment is up?"

"Available now. I met him in Bethesda during my recovery. I'm sure he'd be interested."

"Pass on his details, and I'll contact him."

"And Montana, thanks for the opportunity." Swede held out his hand.

Montana took it and pulled the big man into a bear hug. "We're in this together."

Swede hugged him back. "Once a SEAL, always a SEAL."

"Right. We just have to find out where we fit now that we're not fighting wars in foreign countries."

"If you're going to follow Allie, you'd better get going," Sadie said. "She's pulling down the drive now."

Swede sprinted from the room, feeling only a slight twinge in his thigh from the shrapnel wounds. He hurried to his truck, parked in front of the house. Ruger barked a greeting and moved out of the driver's seat.

"Good boy." Swede started the engine and spun the truck around, spitting gravel in his wake.

ALLIE WAS furious Damien hadn't asked her first before contacting her brother about a bodyguard. She'd made it perfectly clear to her fiancé that she was a very independent woman who liked doing things her way. If he wasn't okay with that, he shouldn't have dated her or asked her to marry him. She wasn't changing for any man.

A glance in her rearview mirror made her smile. She'd left without waiting for Swede. If he was to be her bodyguard, he'd have to do a whole lot better at keeping up.

He didn't catch up to Allie until she slowed to turn onto the highway.

Yes, she was driving like a bat out of hell, racing along the highway like she was actually trying to lose him. Maybe she was. Having someone follow her around like she needed a babysitter wasn't her idea. Why make it easy on the man?

Apparently, Swede wasn't so easily deterred. He caught up and rode her tail, even though she was breaking the speed limit.

The gate to her current home with her father at Bear Creek Ranch came and went. She didn't slow down until she reached the grandiose stone and wood monstrosity with the words Double Diamond Ranch seared into the cedar archway. Unlike most gravel ranch roads, the Double Diamond road was paved all the way up to a huge mansion of a house, spreading across the top of a knoll.

Damien had purchased it from a movie star who'd gotten tired of the cold winters and moved back to sunny California to retire. The drive was lined with trim white wood fencing and trees spaced perfectly along the way. Horses grazed in the pastures if they weren't being cared for in the massive stable. The stable was magnificent with twelve stalls, a spotless tack room and an office for the foreman.

Allie had a love-hate relationship with the ranch. She loved what wealth could buy, but, at the same time, hated the waste of so many dollars on things that weren't necessary to have a working ranch in Montana. But, this wasn't a working ranch. It was a gentleman's retreat where riding was done for exercise and fun, not out of the necessity of managing cattle.

When she married Damien, she hoped to change that. She wasn't the kind of woman who sat around the house eating bon bons with servants who tended to her every need. *Bleck!* She got the sour taste in her mouth, and felt the need to spit to clear it.

Allie pulled to a stop in front of the mansion and slid out of the driver's seat. Without waiting for Swede, she marched up to the front entrance and pounded on the door, her anger fueling her fist.

Footsteps sounded on the steps behind her. The bodyguard was getting faster. Darn it all.

A man in a uniform opened the door. "Ah, Miss Patterson. Mr. Reynolds is out at the stable. Perhaps you'd like to come inside and wait for him?"

"No, thank you, Miles. I'll find him." Allie turned and ran into Swede. Beside him was a blue merle Australian shepherd with ice blue eyes much like his master's. "Why are you standing so close?"

He stepped aside with what could only be regarded as a sarcastic flourish. "Maybe if you looked before you rushed headlong into things, you wouldn't have a problem with where I stand."

She snorted. "This your sidekick?"

"You could say that. His name is Ruger."

Her expression softened, and she reached down to scratch the dog's ears. She had a soft spot for dogs, especially working dogs, which she was almost sure this one was not.

Ruger leaned against her leg, his tail thumping against the stoop.

Allie could get lost in eyes so blue. Her jaw hardened, she straightened and gave Swede a narrow-eyed glare. "Just stay out of my way, will ya?" She ducked around him and marched across the manicured lawn toward the stable. "Damien!" she called out. "I need to talk to you."

Her fiancé, dressed in freshly pressed khaki slacks, a dark polo shirt, and black leather jacket emerged from around the far side of the stable, his brows pulled into a deep frown. "Alyssa, what are you doing here?"

Not '*Alyssa, darling, I'm so happy you came to see me*'. Was the honeymoon over before it had even begun? And without the requisite sex? That was another thing she would take up with Damien when she had a moment alone with him. Why hadn't they gone all the way yet? This waiting for the wedding bullshit was positively archaic. What if he was lousy in bed? Worse yet, what if she was lousy in bed with him? She wasn't a virgin, but it had been a while since she'd slept with someone.

Frustrated by all she had to do before the wedding and adding the aggravation of having to put up with a shadow following her around, she launched her attack.

"What's this about you going behind my back to hire a bodyguard for me?"

He glanced back in the direction from where he'd come. "Darling, I think it's best. It appears that I've made a few enemies along the road to success. Some would like to steal away my good fortune."

"What kind of enemies?" Swede asked, stepping up beside Allie. He held out his hand. "I'm the bodyguard you hired. Axel Svenson. Most people call me Swede."

Allie crossed her arms over her chest as the men shook hands.

"Damien Reynolds. I'm glad to meet you. Let me show you the latest in what has me concerned." He hooked Allie's elbow, turned and walked around the side of the stable. He stopped and waved his hand at the wall. Splashed across the side of the well-maintained structure were bold letters spray-painted in red.

TAKE WHAT'S MINE

I'LL TAKE WHAT'S YOURS

A chill slithered down Allie's spine at how the red paint resembled blood, with long trails dripping from the letters down the side of the stable. She shuddered and straightened. "Damien, it's just paint."

His mouth pressed into a thin line. "It's a threat. A promise to take what I've accumulated here. Whoever did this might also target the people I care about."

Swede turned to Allie. "Didn't your brother say something about cut brake lines on your truck?"

Damien's brows dipped. "Have you had anything else happen since then?"

Allie shot a narrow-eyed glare at Swede. "No. And that could have been a fluke."

"I'd rather be safe than sorry. Less than a week remains until our wedding. Then we'll get away on our honeymoon, and leave all of this behind."

"If there really is a problem," Allie pointed to the stable wall, "which it seems there is, we'd only delay dealing with the issue."

Damien shoved a hand through his immaculate hair. The gesture barely ruffled the dark locks.

Sometimes that irritated Allie, considering she looked like she needed to brush her hair the minute she stepped outside.

"How about us tackling one challenge at a time?" He lifted her hand and pressed a kiss to her callused fingers. "Let Mr. Svenson get you to the wedding on time and intact. When we get back from the honeymoon, we can deal with whoever is causing the problems."

"I can take care of myself," Allie insisted. "I have a gun, and I know how to use it."

"I know you do, darling. But you can't always be watching over your shoulder. I know you have last-minute preparations for the wedding. You don't need to worry yourself about some lunatic stirring up trouble. Leave it to your bodyguard."

Allie bristled, biting hard on her tongue. One of the things she liked about Damien was also one of the attributes that really pissed her off. He treated her like a lady. As a hardcore rancher, it was a nice change to be seen as a woman, not just another ranch hand. But then,

Damien sometimes took it a little too far, treating her like a woman who didn't know one end of the gun barrel from the other. Rather than call him on his patronizing attitude, and show any discord between them to the hired bodyguard, Allie swallowed the words she wanted to say. "Okay, I'll let him tag along."

"Good, because I have to go out of town for the next few days."

Allie frowned. "Our wedding is in less than a week. You promised you'd be here to help with last-minute details."

"Now, Alyssa, I still have a business to run. I can't just let it go." He glanced at the stable wall. "Some emergencies have come up and I need to handle them."

"Fine," she said. "Just be sure to make it to the church on time for the rehearsal and the actual ceremony." She'd be damned if she got stood up at the altar like some pathetic female in a romance novel. In this case, she'd have to get in line behind her father and brother to shoot him. "When are you leaving?"

"This evening. I'm catching a flight out of Bozeman." He cupped the back of her head and bent to kiss her.

As soon as his lips touched hers, an explosion rocked the earth beneath Allie's feet. Damien dropped where he stood.

Swede grabbed Allie and threw her on the ground, covering her body with his as a second explosion blasted through the side of the stable, shooting splintered boards over their heads.

Fire shot up from the far end of the stable, and

smoke filled the air. Horses screamed inside the remaining walls. Ruger barked in response.

Allie bucked beneath Swede. "Let me up!"

Swede rolled to the side, and pushed to his feet.

As soon as his heavy weight was off her, Allie jumped up and ran into the burning building.

CHAPTER 2

SWEDE RACED AFTER ALLIE, his body shaking, the explosion having thrown him back to his combat days. Only this wasn't Afghanistan or Iraq. His primary job was to protect a woman hell-bent on running headfirst into danger.

Seeing Allie run into the burning stable, Swede had no other choice but to chase after her into the smoke-filled structure. Ruger tried to follow, but Swede pointed his finger at the dog's nose. "Stay." He could only pray the dog would remember the one command long enough for Swede to get Allie out.

Inside, the smoke hit him immediately, burning his eyes and lungs. He pulled his T-shirt up over his mouth and blinked to clear his eyes. Hunkering below the bulk of the smoke, he hurried toward the pair of legs encased in blue jeans, standing in front of a stall, struggling to throw open the latch.

A horse on the other side pawed at the gate, its eyes rolled back, nostrils flaring.

Swede brushed aside Allie, slammed the lever to the side and jerked the door open.

With a shrill scream, the horse pushed through and raced toward the exit.

Allie had gone deeper into the smoke-filled stable and threw open another stall.

The horse inside reared, thrashing its legs.

Swede grabbed Allie and dragged her out of the way of the deadly hooves.

"Let go of me!" she cried, struggling to be free.

"Get out, now." Swede coughed and ducked low. "I'll take care of the rest of them."

"No way." Allie's eyes streamed with tears, making tracks in the soot clinging to her face. "One person can't get them all." She pushed away, and ran to the next stall.

Rather than fight her, Swede pitched in and helped her free the remaining horses from the stable. When the stalls were empty, he waved to Allie. "Get out. Now!" The heat from the fire bore down on him, but he wouldn't leave until she was out.

Allie ran for the door and Swede fell in behind her. At the last minute, just before he passed through the open door, a movement caught his eye. He reached between two feed barrels and snagged a cat by the scruff of its neck. With the feline clawing at his arm, Swede dove for the door. Once outside, he didn't let go of the cat until he was far enough away from the stable the cat wouldn't run back inside. When he set the creature on the ground, it ran back toward the stable. Ruger blocked its way, growling fiercely. The cat changed directions and ran toward the house.

ALLIE'S LUNGS burned with every breath. She knelt on the ground fifteen feet from the barn, coughing so hard her entire body shook with the force.

Swede dropped down beside her, his lungs burning, and coughing equally as hard. "We need to get you to a hospital," he said, between fits of hacking. "Smoke inhalation can be fatal."

She raised her hand, swallowed hard and shook her head. "I don't need a hospital. I just need fresh air." Her gaze went to the stable. "What kind of monster targets a stable full of horses? What did the horses ever do to him?"

"Some people have no respect for life," Swede said. "Animal or human."

"People like that need to die a really terrible death." Her chest still tight, Allie lay down on the ground and closed her eyes. A moment later, she sat up straight when a thought came to her. "Where's Damien?"

Swede shook his head. "He wasn't in the stable. I made a final sweep before we got out."

Allie glanced around. "Thankfully, all of the animals survived. When the fire burns down and the horses can be gathered, we can assess injuries."

"Alyssa!" Damien came running from the direction of the house. "Thank God, you're okay. The fire department is on its way."

Allie wanted to ask him where the hell he was when the horses were trapped inside their stalls. The call to the fire department could have waited until all the animals were safe. She stood, brushing the grass and dust off her jeans.

Damien opened his arms for her, but she didn't step into them.

"I'm covered in soot. I wouldn't want to mess up your jacket with the smell."

He glanced down at the garment. "I don't care about the jacket." And he pulled her into his arms. "I'm just glad you're all right." He tipped her face up to him, pulled a cloth handkerchief out of his pocket and dabbed at her lips. Then he kissed her. "You shouldn't have gone into the stable."

"I wasn't about to let those horses burn in the fire."

"But you could have died." He kissed her again and then set her to arm's length. "Now, do you see why I wanted to hire a bodyguard?"

Witnessing the tender moment, Swede turned away from the couple. He'd have to get used to disappearing if he wanted this bodyguard gig to work out. He imagined the first rule of being a bodyguard was to keep one's mouth shut. A good bodyguard was there all the time, but not to be seen or heard, except when necessary. Or at least, that's how he figured it should be. He wondered if Hank had drafted a set of standard operating procedures for the company. He made a mental note to ask the next time he saw his friend.

Ruger leaned against his leg, a low whining sound rising up his throat. Swede bent to pat the dog's head and scratch behind his ears. "It's okay, boy. You did good."

"So, it's all settled then?" Reynolds was saying.

Swede turned back to Allie and her fiancé.

"Mr. Svenson, you're in charge of my bride's safety," Reynolds said. "I expect you to guard her with your life, and make sure she gets to the church for the wedding." He glanced down at Allie. "From what your brother said, this man is one of our nation's finest. A navy SEAL, a combat veteran skilled in almost every weapon imaginable. Who better to guard my precious Alyssa?"

Swede fought to keep from rolling his eyes or snorting. In the brief amount of time he'd known Allie, he could imagine she was fighting not to gag. The woman had spunk and valued her independence. *Precious* wasn't one of the words Swede would use to describe her. It was too frilly.

Allie stepped back. "You be careful, too. You're in more danger than I am. Whoever is mad at you blew up *your* stable, not mine."

Damien nodded, his jaw tightening. "I hope to find out who it is while I'm away, but it pays to be overly cautious, especially after we've seen what he might do. Now, if you'll excuse me, I have to pack a bag and get to the airport. I trust you can answer any questions the fire department might have." Without waiting for a response, the man turned and left Allie and Swede standing in front of the burning stable.

Less than five minutes later, Reynolds drove away in a white Land Rover, before the fire trucks could arrive.

Swede shook his head. The man had narrowly

missed being blown up in an explosion, his fiancée had almost died in the ensuing fire, and he'd been willing to let his expensive horses die. Swede violated his first rule of being a bodyguard and opened his mouth. "You're engaged to him?"

"Don't judge." Allie turned and walked away.

"Right. I'm just the bodyguard," Swede muttered under his breath and followed her. "Where are you going?"

"The horses need to be caught and put out to pasture before the fire truck spooks them and they run out onto the highway." She walked up to a horse standing in the corner of a fence, its eyes wild, its feet dancing in the dirt, stirring up a small cloud of dust.

Allie spoke in a calm voice. "It's okay. That big bad fire won't get you." She slowly reached for the animal's halter.

The gelding reared, pawing at the air, nearly knocking over Allie.

Swede grabbed her around the middle and pulled her out of reach. Only thing was that, once he had her out of harm's way, he didn't want to let go. The woman tried his patience and had a mouth on her, but she cared about the horses and risked her own life to save theirs. He admired that in the infuriating woman.

"What are you doing?" Allie demanded, struggling to free herself from his hold.

When he realized he'd held on too long, he abruptly let go.

Allie broke free and backed away in a hurry. Her

movement startled the gelding. Again, the animal rose on its hind legs.

And, once again, Swede grabbed her and pulled her away from the flailing hooves. This time, she was facing him and her hands rested on his chest.

For a moment, she froze, her fingers curling into his shirt. Her gaze rose from his chest to his mouth.

For a brief, unexplainable moment, Swede had the undeniable urge to kiss the woman.

Her eyes widened, and she pushed against his chest. "Let go of me."

"The horse is understandably afraid. Let me try to catch him." Swede held her a moment longer. "I'm going to release you. Please don't make any sudden moves."

"I know what I'm doing," she insisted with a glare. "I grew up around horses."

"Just let me do this."

"How many horses have you been around?" she asked.

"Counting the ones we got out of the stable?" His lips twisted. "Five." The total number of horses they'd rescued from the fire.

"My point, exactly." Allie pushed her sleeves up her arms. "You'll get hurt."

"Give me the benefit of the doubt," Swede said. "Stay here with Ruger. He's never been around farm animals, that I know of. Keep him from coming after me."

Allie waved an arm. "Fine. Go ahead. Get yourself killed. Then I won't have you following me around." She dropped to her haunches next to Ruger. "Poor dog. What did you do to deserve him?"

"I'll have you know he was on death row at a dog pound when I rescued him." But, if Swede was telling the whole truth, Ruger had been the one doing the rescuing.

Standing in front of the frantic beast with the heat of the still-burning fire behind him, Swede studied the animal. Having grown up in the city, he'd never really thought much about horses. Like most kids, he'd always dreamed of living on a ranch and riding horses, but the opportunity had never presented itself. Now that he was in Montana, he would make a point of learning how to ride and care for a horse.

Starting now.

He eased toward the horse, maintaining eye contact with the beast. When he'd brought Ruger home, he'd treated him with kindness and respect, he noticed how the dog responded to the tone of his voice even when he talked nonsense. If that worked with a dog, perhaps it would work with a horse. He spoke in a low, steady, monotone, advancing slowly, holding out his hand, praying the horse didn't take a bite out of it or trample him in his crazed state of mind. This horse was like most creatures when they were scared, it needed reassurance and comfort.

Swede inched toward the horse, and it whinnied and pawed at the dirt, but it didn't rear. Hoping the smell of smoke wasn't still clinging to his skin, Swede let the horse smell his hand and touch his fingers with its big lips. The sensation was new and exhilarating to Swede. The horse was like a big dog. When he thought of it that way, he relaxed and smoothed his hand over the nose and up to scratch behind his ears, wrapping his other hand around the halter.

ALLIE HATED THAT SWEDE, a greenhorn who'd never been near a horse, had walked up to one who was so clearly spooked and calmed him.

She snorted. "Beginner's luck. We have four more to catch. You better get cracking." She walked with Ruger over to a gate and held it open.

Swede led the animal through and released it on the other side.

The horse galloped across the pasture, moving as far away from the smoke and flames as it could get.

The other four horses were easier to round up, and they soon had all of them in the fenced pasture. Just in time, too. The wailing of sirens grew louder, and soon the driveway filled with a pumper truck, a paramedic's vehicle, and a sheriff's deputy. Several ranchers' trucks arrived, all part of the volunteer firefighters who served the county.

Swede and Allie moved back as the fire-fighters made use of the nearby pond and pumped water onto the flames. Unfortunately, the stable was a complete loss, but the firefighters kept the blaze from spreading to the house and grassy fields.

After the paramedics checked out both Swede and Allie for smoke inhalation, they gave them a blast of oxygen. The pair was released, with the recommendation that they go to the clinic in Eagle Rock.

But, that would have to be later. The sheriff and fire

chief had questions. Allie answered them as best she could. Someone had left a threatening message on the side of the building, and then the building exploded. She had no idea who the perpetrator might be. The only person who might have the answer to that question had left to catch a flight out that afternoon. Yes, he should be back within the week. He had a wedding to attend, after all.

What else could she say? Less than a week out from her wedding, and this incident hit her full in the face. How well did she know her fiancé? She knew so little about his business and why someone would want to hurt him. She swore she'd grill Damien thoroughly before the wedding. How had she been so caught up in her own life she hadn't bothered to get to know her future husband's? Had she thought the man was independently wealthy just because his parents were rich?

For the first time since she'd agreed to marry Damien, Allie started to get cold feet. Up until now, the relationship had seemed like a fairytale. She'd met her prince charming at a local fundraiser for charity. He'd taken her out on several dates, and then flown her in his private jet to have dinner in Seattle. Yeah, he'd swept her off her feet, and shown her a life so foreign she couldn't help but be dazzled. Best of all, he treated her like a woman, instead of another one of the guys.

When he'd popped the question less than a month ago, he'd been so romantic. He'd gotten down on one knee and asked her to marry him. Just like in the movies. It was every girl's dream. Allie had been no different. She couldn't say no to the man, or the life he promised. And his ranch was something she had only fantasized of. She couldn't wait to dig in and make it all it could be, not just a show place.

Hell, was she more in love with the ranch than the man? She shook her head. No. Damien might not know how to be a rancher, but that wasn't why she was marrying him. She cared for him. When she'd had disagreements with her cantankerous father, she'd turned to Damien, who'd been there to just hold her and let her vent. He hadn't offered advice, presumably because he trusted her judgment on how to handle her family.

He was an excellent horseman, having ridden in competitive dressage since he was a teenager. His parents had spared no expense in his education, sending him to private schools and then Yale. As a child, he'd traveled all over the world, and then again for the business he'd built for himself in contracting.

The tension slowly released from her shoulders. Maybe she knew more about him than she thought. So, she didn't know the particulars about his contracting business, only that he made a lot of money doing it. He had building projects all over the world, with a concentration in the rebuilding efforts going on in Afghanistan. He'd been there twice already that year, and maybe he was headed there now. When he called to check in, she'd ask.

A pickup pulled in behind the fire truck and emergency vehicles. Will Franklin got out, his eyes rounding. He walked up to where Allie and Swede stood near the sheriff and the fire chief. "What happened?" he asked.

Allie filled him in on the explosion.

Will started toward the stables. "The horses?"

Placing a hand on the man's arm, Allie answered, "Swede and I got them out." She turned to her bodyguard. "This is Will Franklin, Damien's foreman. Will, this is Swede Svenson. A...friend of mine."

Will shook hands with Swede and then glanced around. "Where's Mr. Reynolds?"

"He left shortly after the explosion," Allie said. "Apparently, he had to take care of business before the wedding."

"I'd better check the horses."

"I'll help." Allie followed Will through the gate to the pasture.

Swede followed with Ruger trotting alongside.

The horse he'd sweet-talked came trotting up to him.

Grinning, Swede held out his hand, and the horse nuzzled his open palm.

"Has he been around horses much?" Will asked Allie.

"No." Allie shook her head.

Will's lips twisted and he shook his head. "That horse doesn't usually come up to anyone."

Swede held the gelding's halter while Will and Allie looked over the animal. Other than smelling like soot, he seemed to be okay.

They performed the same inspection on the other four horses. When Will and Allie were satisfied they hadn't suffered any lasting ill effects, Allie checked in with the fire chief and sheriff once more.

ELLE JAMES

"If you need us for further questions, we'll be at the Bear Creek Ranch."

Without waiting for her escort, she crossed to her truck, climbed in and left the Double Diamond.

Swede, with Ruger, stayed right behind her all the way to the ranch house.

As Allie drove up to her family home, she wondered what sleeping arrangements she'd have to make for her new bodyguard. She snorted. Her father would be thrilled to know she was bringing a man into his house. As her bodyguard, he couldn't sleep in the barn. Nor could he sleep in the foreman's quarters, as that was already taken. Unlike larger ranches, they didn't have a bunkhouse for ranch hands. It was up to her, her father, and Eddy, their foreman, to manage the herd. During cattle roundup days, they hired extra hands who slept in the barn, and Mrs. Edwards cooked for them.

No, Swede would have to stay in her brother's old bedroom. A tingle rippled down her spine at the thought of the big SEAL sleeping in the room next to her. But then, he was a bodyguard. What good was a bodyguard if he wasn't close to the body he was guarding?

She parked the truck beside the old house with its wide porches. Yeah, the paint was peeling and the steps needed repair, but the place was her home. At least, for the next week. Allie's heart squeezed in her chest. It wasn't as big and fancy as the mansion at the Double Diamond, but it had a helluva view of the Crazy Mountains, and it had been the house where she'd lived for the past twenty-seven years.

Allie supposed she'd get used to living on the Double Diamond. She'd be with Damien, when he was home from his trips. She'd have Miles, the butler, and Barbara, the cook, to talk to in the big house. She'd spend most of her time outside, tending horses and the cattle she hoped to bring onto the three-thousand-acre ranch.

She opened the door to her truck, pushing aside thoughts of her future home. First things first. Her father couldn't know Swede was her bodyguard. He'd flip if he knew Damien was having trouble. Her father would find out soon enough when word got around about the explosion and fire that consumed the stable at the Double Diamond.

Swede parked beside her, got out and rounded the front of his truck with Ruger.

"I think I can get a room in the house for you, but my father isn't keen on dogs inside."

He glanced at the porch. "Which room is yours? I can toss a sleeping bag outside your window."

"Seriously?" Allie shook her head. "I can't ask you to do that. I'll see what I can do to bend my father's rule."

"I'm not here to cause you more problems. I'm here to keep you safe. And I've slept in worse places than on a porch."

As a SEAL, he probably had. Still… "You can have Hank's old room. Grab your stuff, you can stow it inside." Allie started up the steps. When she realized Swede wasn't following, she turned back to him. "You and Ruger can have Hank's old room. There. Are you satisfied?"

Swede walked around to the side of his truck,

grabbed a duffle bag and an old blanket and followed her into the house.

"Georgia?" Allie called out.

A gray-haired woman wearing jeans and a short-sleeved plaid shirt stepped into the hallway. "Allie, I'm glad you're here. I heard there was a fire out at the Double Diamond, and I was worried you might be there." She studied Allie before hurrying forward and hugging her. "Oh, dear. You were, weren't you? You're all covered in soot and smell like smoke. I'm glad you're okay. What a terrible thing."

Allie almost laughed. News traveled fast in small communities. She should have known it had already made it home. "Do Dad and Eddy know?"

"Not yet. They've been out repairing fences all day. I haven't seen them since breakfast."

Good. She'd get Swede installed before they got back. "Georgia, this is Swede Svenson, a friend of mine from college, who came early for the wedding. He was going to stay in Eagle Rock, but I told him we had room here for him and his dog."

Georgia smiled at Swede and held out her hand. "Nice to meet you. There are fresh sheets on the bed in Hank's old room." Her smile wrinkled into a bit of a frown. "As for the dog, well, you'll have to take it up with Mr. Patterson. He doesn't like animals in the house."

Allie nodded. "I'll take care of it. Could you show him to the room so he can toss his bag? I need to ride out and check on that sick heifer."

"I'm coming with you," Swede insisted.

Allie sighed. "Fine. I'll wait." Again, she didn't want everyone to know Damien had hired a bodyguard. In order to keep that little bit of information on the down-low, she had to play the hostess to her "friend."

This bodyguard business was going to be a big pain in the ass. And having a hunky SEAL following her around might be more difficult than she ever imagined.

CHAPTER 3

SWEDE FOLLOWED Georgia up the stairs and across a landing to the first door on the right.

"You can use this room. The one next to it is Allie's, and at the end of the hall is Mr. Patterson's." She opened the door and stepped aside. "The bathroom is across the hall. If you need anything, let me know. Dinner is at 6:30. Mr. Patterson doesn't like folks being late." She smiled. "Where was it you met Allie, again?"

"In college," he said.

"At Montana State University?" she queried.

He swallowed hard. "Yes, ma'am."

"How did you like Missoula? I have a sister who lives there."

He shrugged. "It's okay," he said, hating that he was lying to a very nice woman. But, Allie had started the lie and he wouldn't be the one to spill the beans.

"Uh-huh." Georgia's eyes narrowed. "And what was your degree?"

"Engineering," he replied. At least this was the truth. Working on his degree online and in a classroom the semesters he was Stateside, he'd earned a degree in engineering. He dropped his bag on the floor and turned to leave the room, only to find Georgia standing in the doorway with her arms folded over her chest.

"How long have you known Allie?" An eyebrow cocked high.

"Five, maybe six…If you don't mind, she's waiting for me." He started toward the woman.

She didn't budge for a moment and then snorted. "Uh-huh." Georgia stepped out of the way. "Remember, supper's on the table at 6:30."

He hurried past her and down the stairs. Ruger fell in step beside him as he pushed through the door onto the porch where he found Allie.

"Is there a reason you lied to Georgia about who I am?" he asked, his voice terse, anger simmering low in his belly.

Allie glanced at the house where Georgia stood in the window of the kitchen, watching them. "I didn't want them to worry about me."

"Well, you need to tell me more about yourself before you commit me to being an old school chum. In what city is Montana State University?"

"Bozeman."

Damn. "Not Missoula?"

"No. That's University of Montana."

He winced. "You'll have to do some damage control with Georgia. She's on to me." He left it at that and walked down the steps.

"I'll square up with her before dinner."

"Which is at 6:30 sharp. She told me twice. I take it that you don't want to be late."

Allie caught up with him and fell in step. "Welcome to the Bear Creek Ranch. My father likes things the way he likes things."

"And he likes the man you've chosen to marry?"

Allie's steps faltered for a moment. "That's none of your business."

"While I'm your bodyguard, everything about you is my business."

"The hell it is." Allie walked faster. She reached the barn first, and turned to face him. "Remember, it wasn't my idea to hire you. If I had my way, I'd have you sent back to the White Oak with Hank, looking for some rich celebrity to follow around like a lap dog." She shot a glance at the animal beside him. "No offense, Ruger."

She spun toward the door and reached for the handle.

Swede slammed his palm onto the wood, keeping the door from budging. "Look, princess, as long as I'm being paid to protect you, I'm following you around like a lap dog. Only, this lap dog bites. So don't push me."

She turned in the small amount of space between the barn door and his chest and stared up into his eyes. "I'm not a princess, and if you call me that again, I'll show you just how not a princess I can be. Now, move your arm." Her green eyes flashed and color rose in her cheeks.

God, she was beautiful and fearless. Swede had scared newbie SEALs with his full-on glare. Not this ranch woman with fire in her eyes and bright auburn hair. He held his ground for another second, his pulse pounding and his breath mingling with hers, fighting that sudden desire to kiss her.

Her eyes widened and she licked her lips.

As though she could read his mind.

As soon as the thought struck, he dropped his arm and moved away.

Allie lifted her chin, turned and ducked into the barn.

Swede followed at a slower pace, wondering what the hell was wrong with him? Bodyguards weren't supposed to kiss their clients. Especially one who'd told him multiple times she didn't want him around. He found her in the tack room, a blanket and bridle over one shoulder as she hefted a saddle from a wooden stand.

"Here, let me," Swede said, because his mother had raised a gentleman, and gentlemen lifted heavy objects for ladies.

He reached for the saddle.

But, she jerked away. "You'll need to get your own."

He glanced around the room at the seven saddles resting on stands. "Which would you suggest?"

Her lips twitched, and she tilted her head to get a look at his backside. "One big enough for your butt."

His groin tightened at her playful look. Immediately, he turned away before he started thinking about her as anything other than the person he was assigned to protect, who happened to be engaged to the man who'd hired him. At first glance, the saddles all looked pretty much the same. Upon closer inspection, he selected a dark brown one he hoped would fit, grabbed a blanket from a stack and hurried out of the tack room.

Allie had her horse tethered outside a stall. She'd already placed the blanket and saddle on the horse and was reaching beneath the horse's belly for the girth.

Swede knew what these were because, as a kid, he'd dreamed of learning to ride and studied what he could find in his grade school library. He watched carefully as she looped a long leather strap through the metal ring on the girth, pulled it tight, and then looped it again. When she'd used most of the strap, she tied the remainder in a single knot. Then she let the stirrup down.

"Is there a particular horse you want me to ride?" he asked.

She gave him an assessing glance. "Little Joe. Last stall on the left. You get the horse and I'll get his bridle."

Swede walked to the last stall on the left and opened the gate. The horse nudged his way through and would have taken off, but Swede slipped his hand through the animal's halter before he'd gone two steps and brought him under control. He spoke to the horse like he'd done with the spooked one at the Double Diamond. Within seconds, he was able to walk him to the spot next to Allie's horse where a lead rope was tied to a metal loop. He snapped the lead on the halter and quickly laid the blanket and saddle in place. Then he reached beneath the horse and pulled the girth up, looping the leather through the ring, like he'd seen her do.

"Make sure you get it tight. Little Joe likes to blow

out his belly while you're saddling him. And you'll need to adjust the stirrups to fit your longer legs."

Following her advice, he tightened the girth and adjusted the stirrups, while Allie slipped the bridle into the horse's mouth.

Once they were out of the barn, Allie led her horse to a gate, opened it and waited for Swede to walk his horse through. She followed and closed the gate behind them.

Then she swung up into the saddle from the left side of the horse. As he'd told her, he was very observant. He mimicked every one of her moves until he found himself up in the saddle. Then the horse danced sideways, whinnied and took off running as fast as the goddamn wind. Where were the damned brakes?

Swede held onto the reins and the saddle horn and sent a desperate prayer to the heavens. He'd almost rather be shot at by a dozen Taliban than be at the mercy of a crazed horse. Over the thunder of his horse's hooves and blood pounding in his ears, he heard a shout.

"Whoa!" Allie, atop her mare, raced up beside him, leaned dangerously toward Swede, grabbed the rein closest to her and pulled back. "Whoa!"

Both horses slowed until they came to a halt. Allie handed back the rein and shook her head. "You really haven't ridden a horse before, have you?"

His heart still pounding, he shook his head. "Never." He wiped the sweat off his brow and breathed. "But I learn quickly."

"Tap the flanks with your heels, gently, to make him

go. Pull back on the reins to make him stop." She demonstrated as she spoke. "If pulling back on the reins doesn't do the trick, the horse might have the bit between his teeth. Then you pull back on one side only and make him turn in a circle until he stops."

Swede nodded. "Got it."

"Now, I really need to check on that heifer." She tapped her heels against her horse's flanks, and the animal lurched forward.

Swede did the same.

Little Joe leaped after the other horse.

Swede slipped backward in the saddle, but he righted himself and rode after Allie. Several times, he slowed the horse by pulling back on the reins. The animal didn't like being left behind, but he slowed. Feeling a little more confident, he settled into the rhythm of the horse's gallop. Thankfully, Little Joe was perfectly happy following Allie, giving Swede the opportunity to relax and look around.

The Crazy Mountains were undeniably beautiful, with towering trees and jagged peaks capped with remnants of winter snow clinging to the higher elevations.

Allie led him through a narrow valley, across a stream, up and over a ridge, and then stopped near a copse of trees overlooking a grassy valley.

Swede rode up next to her, pulling back on the reins.

She nodded toward several cows grazing in the field beyond. "She seems to be doing better today. At least she's up and eating."

They all looked pretty healthy to Swede. "Which one is she?"

"The brown and white Hereford at the edge of the others." Allie pointed to one that was a bit smaller and not as filled out. "She's okay, for now. I'll check on her tomorrow."

Allie glanced across at Swede. "How are you?"

"Fine." He shifted in the saddle, knowing he'd be sore later. But he'd never admit it to her.

"Trotting is the hardest gait on the butt. If you stand up in your stirrups every other bump, you won't be beaten to death. It's called posting. Like this." She tapped her horse's flanks and the animal took off at a trot. Allie rose and fell in rhythm with the horse's steps.

Swede nudged his mount and the horse broke into a trot. He tried what Allie demonstrated, but ended up standing in the stirrups the entire time, not quite getting the rhythm.

"When you get it right, it stops hurting," she said. "Then the movement becomes natural."

"How long have you been riding?" he asked.

"Since I was big enough to sit up on my own, so my father says. I think I was about four years old when my father put me on a horse by myself." Squinting in the sun, Allie turned back in the direction from which they'd come. "It's getting close to dinner time. We'd better get back."

They crossed the ridge and eased down the other side into the narrow valley with a stream winding through. Everything seemed so peaceful and different than the hills of Afghanistan, filled with Taliban fighters waiting to blow off his head.

Just when Swede thought it couldn't get more placid, the roar of a small engine echoed off the hillsides.

Swede looked around for the source, but the echoes made it hard to determine. Then a four-wheeled all-terrain vehicle erupted out of the tree line and raced straight for Allie.

Swede urged his horse forward, creating a barrier between the oncoming vehicle and the woman he was supposed to protect. He reached beneath his jacket and pulled out the nine millimeter Glock he'd purchased before he'd left the military and aimed for the man on the ATV. He'd give him five more seconds to turn away.

Five. Four. Three. Two. One.

Just as Swede pulled the trigger, he saw Allie's horse rear, throwing her from the saddle. Spooked by Allie's horse and the oncoming ATV, Little Joe bucked.

Swede's shot went wide of its target.

The sound was enough to make the rider swerve to the right and cross the stream, heading up into the hills.

Swede yanked the reins, turned the horse and trotted back to where Allie lay on the ground, her own horse long gone.

The woman lay perfectly still, her eyes wide open.

Swede started to dismount when Allie said, "Don't move."

"Why? Are you okay?"

"I will be, as long as you don't move a muscle and keep Little Joe from coming any closer."

Then he heard the telltale buzz of a rattlesnake's tail.

Wound into a tight coil, lying in the dirt near a rock, lay the biggest rattlesnake Swede had ever seen.

The slightest move on Allie's part could make the snake strike her in the face.

"Be very still," he advised.

"Duh. You think I don't know that?" she said, barely moving her lips and whispering softly so as not to disturb the creature.

"I'll slide down off the horse."

"Any movement could make him strike. I'd rather you didn't."

"What do you want me to do?"

"I don't know. Feed him a mouse. Wait until he leaves. Shoot him. Something." Her voice was soft and calm for having a huge snake in her face.

Little Joe appeared unfazed by the snake lying nearby. He stood still, waiting for Swede's next command.

Still holding the nine-millimeter in his hand, he raised it and aimed down the barrel at the snake.

"What are you doing?" Allie said, through gritted teeth.

"Close your eyes," he said.

"Oh, no, you are not…" She squeezed her eyes shut and tensed.

Swede pulled the trigger. The bullet hit the snake in the head, flipping it over in the dust.

Little Joe danced to the side, but didn't bolt.

Allie rolled away and jumped to her feet. "Are you crazy?"

Swede holstered his weapon and dropped down out

of the saddle. Holding onto the reins, he approached Allie and gripped her arm. "Are you okay?"

"I'm fine, despite the fact you could have killed me."

"But, I didn't." He looked into her eyes, checking her pupils. "Did you bang your head against the ground?"

Allie rubbed her bottom. "No, I hurt my pride more than anything else. I haven't been thrown from a horse in years." She glanced at the snake lying still on the ground. "I guess Major had a good reason to spook." Brushing the dust off her jeans, she looked out across the stream and up the hill on the other side. "Who the hell was on the ATV?"

"I was hoping you could tell me."

"It wasn't one of our vehicles."

"He was aiming for you. And I was aiming for him when your horse reared."

Allie frowned. "I guess I should thank you."

"No need. I was just doing my job."

"Okay, so you aren't a great horseman, but you did shoot the snake without killing me." She drew in a deep breath and let it out. "Thanks."

"You're welcome."

"Now, we'd better get back to the house before we're late for dinner."

Allie balanced her hands on her hips. "Since my horse is halfway back to the barn by now, we'll have to ride double. I'll drive. But you'll need to mount first."

Swede swung up into the saddle, removed his foot from the stirrup and reached for her hand.

Allie placed her toe where his had been, and Swede

pulled her up in front of him. For a moment, she was sitting in his lap. Her auburn hair drifted into his face.

Inhaling a hint of strawberry and the fresh, outdoor scent clinging to her, he closed his eyes and tried not to think of her sitting where she was, or that his groin was reacting naturally and hardening.

His eyes snapped open and he pushed backward, over the lip of the saddle and sat on Little Joe's rump.

He tried holding onto the saddle, but as soon as Allie nudged Little Joe's flanks, the animal leaped forward.

Swede slipped backward and almost fell off the horse. He wrapped his arms around Allie's waist and held tight all the way back to the barn.

When they arrived in the barnyard, Swede slipped off the back of the horse and landed on his feet.

Allie swung her leg over Little Joe's back, and dropped to the ground. "You didn't do badly for your first ride on a horse."

The insides of his thighs ached, but it was a good ache. After months in a hospital and physical therapy, getting out into the open, clean air of Montana felt good.

Now, if he could keep Allie safe from whoever just tried to run her over, he'd feel even better.

ALLIE HURRIED into the house to get cleaned up and dressed for dinner. Her father believed in punctuality. As children, if they weren't at the table on time, they didn't eat. Of course, when their mother was alive, she'd sneak a snack into their rooms, later. After she'd passed away, Georgia continued the tradition.

When Allie got married and had her own house, she wouldn't be as strict. She might even have dinner at different hours other than 6:30pm every single day. She ran up the stairs, calling out, "I have the shower first."

A low chuckle sounded at the bottom of the stairs, warming her from the inside.

When she made it to the top, she glanced over the banister.

Swede stood at the base of the staircase, his hand resting on the banister, staring up at her, his mouth tipped upward in a smile.

Allie stumbled, recovered and ran for her bedroom, her cheeks burning.

The man had no right to be so very handsome when he smiled. And how different from Damien. Not that Damien wasn't handsome. He was. Like a prince. Not like a rugged navy SEAL with boundless muscles and a wicked grin.

Grabbing fresh jeans and a soft green pullover blouse, she entered the bathroom, locked the door and ducked under the shower's cool spray. By the time she'd rinsed off the dirt, smoke and sweat from her body and shampooed her hair, she had her head on straight. Without wasting any time, she was out of the shower, dried and had combed the tangles out of her long hair, thinking for the hundredth time she needed to cut it short. But she couldn't bring herself to do more than trim it. Every time she looked into the mirror, she saw her mother, the parent who'd given her the auburn hair and green eyes her father had fallen in love with.

Dressed and brushed, she ducked back into her room, pulled on socks and a pair of clean boots and ran down the stairs to see if Georgia needed help getting the food on the table. She didn't run into Swede, figuring he was in his room unpacking.

Georgia stood at the stove, stirring gravy in a pot. "You can take the roast out to the table."

Allie did, and returned to the kitchen. "Mmm. That smells good."

Having been the housekeeper since before Allie's mother passed, Georgia was like a surrogate mother. She lifted the pot off the stove and poured the gravy into a bowl. "Before your father comes down, you want to tell me why you lied to me, your father and Eddy?"

With a spoonful of gravy halfway to her mouth, Allie grimaced. "I'm sorry I lied."

"I wasn't born yesterday." Georgia planted a fist on her hip. "Swede didn't go to school with you, did he?"

Allie had hated lying to Georgia. It gnawed at her belly, making her feel nauseated. "No. I met him this morning, at Hank's."

"So, why did you invite a complete stranger to stay in the house?"

"He's a buddy of Hank's from his navy SEAL team. Damien hired him to be my bodyguard until the wedding."

"Bodyguard?" Georgia's brows furrowed. "Does this have anything to do with the fire at his place?"

Allie nodded. "And my cut brake lines. Someone is

mad at Damien and is taking it out on him. Damien thinks he might be targeting me, as well."

"And what do you think?"

She hated to admit it, but… "I think he's right. When I went out to check on the sick heifer, I was almost run over by someone on an ATV. Swede kept that from happening." Allie didn't add that Swede had shot a snake next to her head as well. No use worrying Georgia any more than she already was, based on her deepening frown.

The older woman took her hands. "What has that fiancé gotten you into?"

"I don't know, but he's working on it." Or so she assumed. Why else would he take off before the sheriff and firefighters arrived at his place to put out a fire?

Georgia held her at arm's length. "You know you can back out of the wedding any time between now and the actual ceremony."

Allie smiled at her. "I'm okay. The wedding is going on as planned. Just a few more days, and I'll be a married woman with a house of my own to run."

"You hate household chores."

"Yeah, but I'll have people to do them for me. The way I like them done." Allie pulled Georgia into a quick hug. "Not that you haven't done a terrific job taking care of us all these years. Have I ever said thank you?"

"Yes, dear. You have." Georgia hugged her tight. "We're going to miss you around here."

"I'll only be a couple of miles away."

"Maybe so, but it will seem like a long way to me. I'll be outnumbered by the men."

Allie laughed. "I'm sure you'll keep them in line."

"Are you two going to stand around gabbing or come eat?" Eddy, the ranch foreman and Georgia's husband, entered the kitchen, sniffed and rubbed his belly. "Something smells good."

Georgia stepped back, dabbing her eyes with the hem of her apron. "Did you wash up?" she said, her voice brisk as she turned toward the stove and retrieved a pan full of corn.

"Yes, I did." Eddy sneaked up behind her, pulled her back against his front and nuzzled her neck. "You smell good enough to eat."

Georgia smacked his hands playfully and giggled. "Oh, go on with yourself."

"Not until I get me some sugar."

She set the pan of corn on the stove, turned in his arm and kissed him. "Now, go set the table."

Eddy grinned and smacked her bottom.

"Dang it, Eddy!" Georgia waved a wooden spoon at him. "I'm not above spanking you with this."

"Promises, promises." He fished silverware from a drawer and laid them on the table, whistling as he did.

Allie was used to their playful antics. The childless couple had always been loving and unabashed at showing it in front of others.

"It's 6:30, are we eating or not?" Allie's father entered the big country kitchen, pulled back the chair at the head of the table and sat.

Allie carried the bowl of corn while Georgia brought a basket full of fresh-baked rolls.

"It's 6:25, not 6:30. Remember, Daddy? You always

set your watch five minutes ahead." Allie shot a glance toward the doorway, wondering what was keeping Swede.

Just as she looked that way, he entered the room.

"Pardon me if I kept you waiting."

Allie's father frowned at Swede. "Who the hell are you? And what are you doing in my house?"

For the next hour, Eddy and Mr. Patterson grilled Swede about everything from letting Ruger in the house, to what he knew about horses and cattle, to the types of weapons his team used on special operations.

With admirable patience, Swede answered every question. Eddy and Allie's father seemed satisfied with the man's answers, even when he owned up to knowing nothing about livestock. When the meal was over, he got up like the inquisition hadn't fazed him a bit.

Allie, on the other hand, felt like she'd been run through the wringer. And the worst part was, she'd seen another side of Swede she hadn't wanted to see. A proud military man who'd served his country and now had to figure out how to fit into a life without the SEALs.

He even helped clean the table and wash dishes.

Damn it, if she wasn't careful, she might end up liking the exasperating man.

Tired from a long day, full of stress and trauma, she trudged up the stairs and brushed her teeth. When she exited the bathroom, she ran into Swede. He'd shed his shirt and boots and wore only jeans.

The moisture in Allie's mouth dried as she stared at his broad, muscular chest.

"Are you okay?" Swede asked.

Dragging her eyes upward, she couldn't make her gaze quite reach his eyes, stopping on his full, sexy lips. "I'm fine," she managed to squeak out. Then she dove into her room and slammed the door behind her.

This just would not do. The man was far too attractive to be a bodyguard.

Allie stripped, pulled on an old MSU T-shirt from her college days and crawled into bed, reminding herself that her wedding was only a few days away. Closing her eyes, she tried to picture Damien in a tuxedo, standing at the altar. But the face she saw wasn't Damien's, it was Swede's.

Double damn.

CHAPTER 4

SWEDE WOKE EARLY the next morning after a crappy night's sleep. Thankfully, he hadn't had any of the dreams that had plagued him since he'd left the service. He dressed in sweats, a T-shirt, and tennis shoes and took Ruger outside. Staying within sight of the house, he performed his morning calisthenics—pushups, sit-ups, leg-lifts and more. It paid to stay in shape. Even while he'd been recovering from his wounds in the hospital, he'd done everything he could.

Today, his hand and thighs ached from riding the day before. He stretched his legs and ran to the end of the driveway and back several times before he finally reentered the house.

The smell of bacon lured him to the kitchen where Georgia cooked breakfast. "This will be ready by the time you're out of the shower," she promised.

"Thanks," Swede said. "It smells good." He took the

stairs two at a time, grabbed a pair of clean jeans, and hit the shower.

When he was done, he stepped out of the tub, toweled dry, and tossed the towel to the floor. He was reaching for his jeans when the door swung open. Swede straightened as Allie started in.

When she saw him standing there naked, she widened her eyes and her mouth dropped open. For a long moment she stared. Then her cheeks turned a brilliant red, and she backed out of the doorway. "Pardon me." She pulled the door shut. Through the panel, she said, "Oh, my God."

Swede laughed out loud, and then tried to pull on his jeans over a rock-hard erection. He waited a minute, thinking of everything that could douse his desire, from babies to grandmothers. Nothing seemed to work when the image of Allie's face kept coming to mind. Carefully tucking himself in, he pulled his T-shirt over his head and let it hang down over the ridge of his fly.

He found Allie downstairs in the kitchen with Georgia. Allie didn't look him in the eye, her cheeks still a pretty shade of pink. "My father and Eddy are out cutting hay, so I'm working the barn today. Have you ever mucked a stall?" Finally, she glanced his way.

Swede shook his head, feeling a little inadequate for the job of ranch hand. "No, but I'm game." *As long as I'm near you.*

"I know the task is not part of your job description, so don't feel like you have to."

Swede shot a glance toward Georgia.

The older woman nodded. "I know. I'm just glad

someone is looking out for our girl." She held up a coffee pot. "Coffee?"

"Please," Swede said.

"I still think you should tell Eddy and your father what's going on." Georgia gave Allie a stern look as she poured the steaming brew into two mugs and carried them to the table. "They could be looking out for you, too."

"Absolutely not," Allie said. "My father would do his best to call off the wedding. I've spent too much money on everything, and the event is only a few days away. I pick up my dress tomorrow, and everything is downhill from there."

Georgia raised her brows. "Downhill?"

Allie rolled her eyes and took one of the plates of food from the kitchen counter. "You know what I mean."

"All the preparations are nothing but money and time," Georgia said.

Swede stood quietly, watching the interaction between the two women.

Apparently, Georgia didn't want Allie to marry Damien. Swede wondered why.

Allie ignored Georgia's comment and focused on Swede, her color back to normal, her jaw set in a tight line. "The sooner we get done cleaning the stalls, the sooner we can exercise the horses. After that, we can call it a day. I have to tell you, though, it'll be a long, hard day."

"I'm up for it."

Allie handed him a plate full of eggs, bacon and biscuits. "Eat up."

After breakfast, Swede followed Allie out to the barn. She handed him a pitchfork and pointed to a wheelbarrow. "Tie the horse up outside the stall and start shoveling."

Swede worked through the morning, glad for the physical labor that flexed his muscles and the rich, earthy smell of manure. It beat the scent of diesel smoke and gun powder any day.

Ruger stood guard outside the barn, lying in a patch of sun, watching as Swede and Allie wheeled barrels full of soiled straw out to a pile behind the barn. By noon, they had all the stalls cleaned, the horses brushed, and the chickens and pigs fed.

Georgia had sandwiches waiting when they came inside. Then they were right back out in the sunshine to exercise the horses.

Allie lunged a couple of mares in the corral and then had Swede take over. She watched him, giving tips on how to handle the animal and the lunging rope.

Swede was glad the horse knew what to do. The work wasn't hard. In fact, it had a certain rhythm that bred a sense of calm.

Georgia shouted from the house that Allie had a call from the caterer.

"This horse is about done. You can turn her out into the pasture and then bring out another horse. Just stay clear of Diablo, the black gelding in the last stall. He's a work in progress, and he hasn't quite got the hang of anything."

"Who rides him?"

"No one, yet. Like I said, he's a work in progress. In other words, he's too wild to handle easily." Allie waved at Georgia. "I have to go. No need to follow me. You can keep an eye on the house from the corral, and I really doubt anyone will attack me there."

Swede nodded. She was right. He had a good view of the house and the road leading to it from the corral.

As Allie hurried inside, Swede couldn't help but follow her progress. He told himself it was part of his job, but the truth was the way her hips swayed in her jeans was completely mesmerizing.

The horse he held on a lead tossed her head, pulling Swede back to the task at hand. He walked her through the gate into the pasture and unhooked the lead.

She pranced away and joined the other horses already grazing.

Glancing back at the house and drive, Swede returned to the barn and walked along the stalls, most of which were empty now. One mare stood placidly, watching him as he passed her and walked down the line of stalls to the end.

When they'd been cleaning, Allie had led Diablo in and out. She'd also taken charge of brushing him.

As Swede neared, the animal stuck his head over the top of the gate and nickered.

"So, you're a real ball-buster, are you?" Swede spoke softly and reached out a hand to rub the gelding's nose.

Diablo nuzzled his hand.

"Do you want out?"

The horse pawed at the dirt and tossed his head as if saying *yes*.

"How hard can it be to walk you around a corral?" Swede snapped the lead onto Diablo's halter and opened the stall.

As soon as the latch was free, Diablo hit the door, knocking Swede backward. He staggered and held on tightly to the lunging rope, while being dragged out of the barn by the bolting horse.

When Swede got his feet under himself, he dug his heels into the dirt and slowed the horse.

Diablo reared and jerked the lead, but Swede held steady and started talking. Soon, the horse stopped fighting and settled on all fours.

Ruger stepped up beside Swede as if to show his support.

Diablo lowered his nose to the dog, and the four-legged creatures sniffed each other.

"You're not so bad, just a little spirited." He raised his hand slowly to stroke the horse's nose. "See? I'm not here to hurt you." The gelding tossed his head as if to disagree. "Ruger wouldn't be beside me now if I hurt him. He trusts me because he gave me a chance. I gave him one, too." Swede continued to talk to the horse as he led him into the corral and closed the gate behind him. Still holding the lead close to Diablo's halter, Swede walked the horse around the outer circle. He kept a running monologue going, to calm the animal.

Ruger stood outside the pen. Every time they passed the dog, the horse looked his way.

After walking around the pen for five minutes,

getting the gelding used to the environment, Swede picked up the pace and settled into a slow and steady jog.

Diablo matched his pace and trotted alongside Swede. Slowly, Swede lengthened the lead, still running with the horse, but putting more distance between them. Whenever Diablo slowed, Swede clicked his tongue and jogged faster, encouraging the horse to keep moving. When the lead was long enough and Swede was standing in the middle of the corral, the horse slowed. Swede clicked his tongue, and Diablo broke into a trot.

After several more circles around the corral, Swede let Diablo come to a stop. He pulled in the lead until he could rub the horse's nose. "You're a good boy," Swede soothed, running his hand across the horse's nose and up to scratch his ears. Then he swept his hand along the gelding's neck to his back.

Diablo pawed the earth and whinnied, swaying on his hooves.

Swede scratched the animal's back, side and around to his belly. He moved his hands up to the horse's back again and laid his arms over the top, scratching the other side, while leaning his weight on the animal.

Diablo tossed his head, but didn't move away.

Holding onto the lead rope, Swede grabbed hold of a handful of Diablo's mane and swung his leg over the top of the horse. He leaned forward and wrapped his arms around Diablo's neck, speaking to him the entire time, fully expecting to be thrown, but hoping it wouldn't happen.

Diablo backed up and then moved forward, whinnying.

Ruger whined behind the rails of the corral, capturing the gelding's attention.

Diablo trotted to where the dog stood and lowered his head to sniff.

Swede molded his body to the horse, still rubbing his neck and speaking softly.

Seeing Diablo and Ruger greeting each other with their noses, Swede slipped off the horse's back and patted his neck. "See? It's not as bad as you think."

When Swede straightened, he noticed he had an audience.

"Damnedest thing I've ever seen." Eddy leaned against a corral panel, his arms resting on the top rail.

"That horse doesn't like anyone," Lloyd Patterson said, scratching his head.

"And to beat it all, Swede never rode a horse until yesterday." Allie joined the two men at the fence, a smile tilting the corners of her lips. "You're lucky he didn't take you for a ride."

Swede rubbed Diablo's neck. "I think he just needed a friend." He tipped his head toward Ruger. Diablo and Ruger sniffed at each other. Ruger's tail thumped the ground.

"The man we bought him from said he had another gelding raised with Diablo," Mr. Patterson said.

"You might want to check and see if he still has him," Allie said. "Seems Diablo needs a friend."

"Why? Swede's dog seems to be doing the job," Eddy said.

"And why feed another horse?" her father added. "It's cheaper to feed a dog."

Allie's smile slipped. "Swede and Ruger are only here until after the wedding." She opened the gate. "I think we have one more horse to exercise. Dad, is there anything else you want done before we call it a day?"

"Not a thing. We could use a little help hauling the first cutting of hay the day after tomorrow. It should be dry enough, and we need to get it in before the rain."

As he walked Diablo though the gate, Swede glanced at the bright blue Montana sky. "Is a rainstorm expected?"

Lloyd flexed his shoulder. "I can feel it in my bursitis. If not tomorrow, then the next day. By the end of the week for certain."

"Great. It'll probably rain on my wedding day," Allie muttered

"You can always put it off," her father said. "No need to rush into marriage."

"I'm getting married on Saturday," Allie said, her tone flat but firm.

Mr. Patterson faced his daughter. "If you're going to get married, why Reynolds?"

"Because he asked me, and I said yes."

Lloyd nodded toward Swede. "Why not marry a real man—like a war hero?"

"Dad!" Allie's face burned a bright red. "You don't even know Swede. Besides, who said he wanted to get married in the first place?" She threw her hands in the air. "What did Mom see in you? All I'm getting is a grumpy old man who is stubborn and insensitive."

Her father's face grew rigid, his eyes a stormy gray. "I loved your mother and would have done anything for her. And she loved me, too." He lifted his chin. "Can you say that about Reynolds?"

Swede could feel the tension between father and daughter, as palpable as electricity singeing the air.

"I'm getting married on Saturday. You can come to the wedding and wish me well–or not. But I don't want to hear another negative word about Damien." She stomped into the barn, leaving the men outside, scratching their heads.

"Women," Lloyd grumbled. "Can't live with them… and can't live without them."

"Guess you'll find out in a few days." Eddy pounded Lloyd's back and turned to Swede. "Good job with Diablo. You might have a knack for ranching after all, city boy."

Swede nodded. "Thanks."

Inside the barn, Allie had grabbed a lunging rope, snapped it onto the last mare needing exercise, and led her past Swede and Diablo. "Don't say a word."

Swede grinned. "I wasn't going to."

"My father raised me, but he doesn't know anything about me, or how I feel."

"Maybe he just wants you to be happy."

Allie raised her hand. "I said, don't say a word." She walked out, leading the mare, her lips pressed into a thin line.

Swede chuckled.

"No laughing, either," Allie's voice sounded from just outside the barn door.

Swede fed Diablo and brushed his coat. Ruger lay nearby. It seemed the dog's mere presence had the same calming effect on the horse as it did on Swede. *Go figure.* All Swede knew was that if not for Ruger, he'd still be suffering the effects of his nightmares and breaking out in cold sweats over loud noises. Yeah, he'd pulled Ruger off death row at the pound, but Ruger had pulled Swede out of a life of misery, suffering from PTSD.

Now, if only the dog could perform miracles and dampen the increasing urge Swede felt to kiss the feisty Miss Patterson.

AFTER THE LAST horse had been exercised and all the animals fed, Allie trudged back to the house and sat on the steps to remove her boots. "Thanks for the help."

Swede dropped down beside her and pulled off his boots, as well. He smelled of sweat, hay and manure. Not the kind of smell Allie associated with Damien. Her fiancé never seemed to sweat. Even when they rode horses together, he came back smelling like his after-shave, not the leather and dusty scent of being in the great outdoors.

Allie should prefer the clean scent of aftershave, but leather and dust, to her, was more manly and satisfying.

She drew in a deep breath, trying not to be too obvi-ous. Yeah, Swede smelled like how Allie considered a man should. But then, she wasn't marrying Damien because of his scent.

Then why was she marrying him?

Because he'd asked, and she didn't want to marry any of the local men she'd grown up with. They were too much like brothers, who didn't even consider going anywhere else but Montana or the nearest stock show or rodeo. Some didn't even want to cross the border into Canada, preferring to remain on their ranches where they'd been born, lived all their lives and where they'd die.

"Do you like to travel?" Allie blurted out without thinking.

Swede shrugged. "I do. But some day I hope to have a place to call home. Traveling is all well and good, but roots help you appreciate where you're going. You're lucky you have a place to call home."

"You don't?" Allie wanted to travel, but like Swede said, she liked to have a home base to come back to.

"Not since my folks died. The closest I came were the apartments I rented near the bases where I was stationed. I rarely saw the insides of those places, having deployed often."

"I'm sorry." She pulled off the second boot and set it beside the first. "Where did your parents live?"

"In Minneapolis, Minnesota."

She smiled softly. "So you have a vague idea of what cold winters are like."

"I do. Not as cold as it gets in Montana, but I know my way around snow."

She gave him an assessing glance. "Ever play hockey?"

Swede nodded. "That's how I got this scar." He pointed to the one on his chin."

"And I thought you'd gotten that working as a SEAL."

He shook his head, his glance shifting to his hand, which he lifted to the scar that ran along the side of his face, from his hairline to his cheekbone. "I got this one in Kandahar Province, on my last mission in Afghanistan."

Allie took his hand in hers and studied the jagged scars between his thumb and forefinger. "And these?"

"Syria."

"Does it still hurt?" she traced the jagged scars with the tip of her finger.

He clenched his hand, only closing it halfway. "A little. I haven't gotten full range of motion yet, but don't worry. I can fire a weapon accurately with either hand."

Her eyes widened and she stared into his. "Holy hell. It didn't even dawn on me that you shot that snake with your left hand. Are you even left-handed?"

Swede shook his head. "Not naturally, but I've learned to be since I joined the navy and became a SEAL. It was a challenge to learn to shoot with both hands. Now, I'm glad I did."

Allie felt warmth filter from his hand into hers and up her arm. She let go of him, grabbed her boots and stood. "You can have the shower first."

"You're not going back out?" he asked.

"No. I thought I'd feed Ruger for you, if you like." She bent to scratch the dog's ears. "He's proving to be useful around here."

Swede's lip quirked up in a half-smile. "He's smart and learns quickly."

Allie chuckled. "Like you?"

"I like to think I can do anything I set my mind to."

"I'll give you that. From what I've seen or read about SEAL training, anyone who can make it through to graduation has to have a lot of stamina and fortitude." She glanced toward the house. "You better get going. I'd like to wash the stink off me, too."

Swede grinned. "I never thought I'd say this, but horse manure smells pretty good on you." He winked and held the door open.

She twisted her lips into a crooked smile. "Thanks. I think."

"Ruger's food is in the mud room," Swede said. Then he turned to the dog. "Stay."

Ruger sat on the porch and whined softly.

"I'll be right back with food and water for you," Allie said, and followed Swede inside.

Swede set his dirty boots inside the mudroom door and headed for the stairs.

Allie set her boots on the floor and straightened, her gaze following the man up the stairs. He had a great butt that looked exceptional in jeans. And he didn't wear fancy, expensive jeans like Damien. Swede wore the kind most of the cowboys around Eagle Rock wore. Plain, serviceable and tough. Like the man. Well, he wasn't exactly plain.

His face wasn't classicly handsome like Damien's, with all his features completely symmetrical. Swede's nose must have been broken more than once and didn't sit exactly straight on his face. He had the scar on his chin, and the one on the side of his face, marring his otherwise rugged good looks. It was the breadth of his shoulders, the trimness of his waist, and the thickness of his thighs that made Allie's heartbeat flutter.

Damn! There she went again. Thinking about the SEAL, rather than dreaming about her future husband.

She picked up Ruger's water bowl, strode into the kitchen and filled it. When she came back out on the deck, the dog sat exactly where Swede had told him to stay. His tail thumped against the porch boards.

Allie set the water in front of Ruger and went back inside for his food. When she came out, she saw he'd lapped up every drop of the water. Then he wolfed down the food she put in front of him, and looked up at her expectantly.

"More?" Allie laughed and gave him more.

When he was finished, she let him into the house.

The telephone rang on the stand in the hallway. Allie answered. "Bear Creek Ranch."

"Allie, Hank here."

"Hey," she said, always glad to hear from her brother since he'd returned from the war in Afghanistan. "What's up?"

"Sadie and I are going out to the Blue Moose Tavern tonight for some drinks and dancing. We thought you and Swede might want to join us."

Allie frowned. Not *you and Damien*. But then, Damien was out of town, and Hank knew it from the fire. She sighed. "Sounds good." She arranged for the time and place to meet and then ended the call.

She'd almost said no. After a hard day's work, she wasn't sure she had the energy to drink and dance. But, it did break the monotony of ranch life. Allie sniffed. First, a shower.

Allie headed upstairs.

Ruger followed and plopped down in front of the bathroom door to wait for Swede. "Traitor. I fed you, he didn't."

The dog stared up at her through soulful blue eyes.

"Fine. Stay here. See if I care."

The door opened, and Swede stood there with a towel looped around his bare shoulders, his wet hair slicked back and wearing nothing but blue jeans, half buttoned up.

The air caught in Allie's lungs, and she fought to push some past her vocal cords. When she finally did, she said, "Fed your dog."

"Thank you. I'm sure Ruger appreciated that." Swede smiled with that melt-me-to-the-core twist of his lips. "Your turn."

Allie had to really focus to make sense of what he was saying. When she did, she nodded. "Great." Then she spun on her socks and ran for her bedroom, where she pressed her palms to her burning cheeks. "What is wrong with me?" she whispered. Then she remembered.

"Oh, Swede?"

The man leaned into the doorway. "Yes, darlin'?"

Don't do that!

She gulped to swallow past the constriction in her throat. "I'm going to meet Hank and Sadie at the Blue Moose Tavern for drinks after dinner."

"Sounds good. What's the dress code?"

"Dress code?" Allie laughed. "We're in Montana, not

the military." She laughed, shut her door and leaned against it. She never laughed like that with Damien.

Why was she suddenly comparing everyone to Damien?

Not everyone. Just Swede.

Damn.

CHAPTER 5

SWEDE DRESSED IN CLEAN JEANS, a white, button-down shirt, and his best cowboy boots he'd purchased before moving west to work in Montana. He didn't know why he hadn't owned a pair before. They were comfortable and easy to get into.

He stood at the bottom of the stairs waiting for Allie to come down. They'd had dinner with Lloyd and the Edwards. After dinner, Allie excused herself to get dressed for their night out with her brother.

Swede didn't see anything wrong with the jeans and T-shirt she'd worn. And her hair, though wet from her shower, was neatly combed and smelled like strawberries. Nope. He didn't see anything wrong with that.

Ruger would remain out on the porch until they returned from the bar. No use keeping him up with loud music. Besides, they might not allow dogs inside.

Georgia stepped into the hallway, wiping her hands on her apron. "My, don't you look nice?"

ELLE JAMES

"Thank you, ma'am," Swede said.

She untied the apron in the back and lifted the strap up over her head. "I was about to leave and go to our house. Is there anything you need before I call it a night?"

"No, ma'am," he answered.

Georgia glanced up the staircase. "There you are. You've kept this man waiting long enough." The older woman smiled. "I'm sure he'll agree it was worth it."

Swede followed Georgia's gaze, his eyes widening, a low whistle escaping from his lips. "Wow."

Allie wore a short white dress that caressed her body perfectly, the skirt brushing against the middle of her thighs with every step she took. She'd dried her hair and it lay in big, soft curls around her shoulders, framing her face. The makeup she'd applied naturally enhanced her cheeks and made her green eyes stand out.

"Wow," he repeated.

Her lips quirked. "You said that." She came down the steps in strappy sandals that drew attention to her toned and tanned calves.

Swede struggled to pull his jaw off the floor and act like a bodyguard, not a teenager on his first date. He couldn't help but look at her several times as if she weren't real, but a figment of his imagination. She was stunningly beautiful in a fresh, girl-next-door way.

"Well, I must say that dress is you." Georgia took her hands and smiled, her eyes misting. "Isn't it one you bought for your honeymoon to the Cayman Islands?"

Allie shrugged. "I felt like wearing it. After all, I'll be

out in public with Sadie McClain. Not that I can compete with her. She's amazing."

"Sweetie, you don't have to compete," Georgia said. "You're beautiful in your own way."

"Thanks." Allie hugged Georgia and then turned toward Swede, her shoulders thrown back, making her breasts rise. "Ready?"

Swede was almost certain he wasn't ready to take Allie for a night on the town. Thankfully, it was only to Eagle Rock, a village with a population of maybe a thousand, counting all of the outlying ranch owners, ranch hands and hound dogs. Surely they'd roll up the sidewalks by 9:00.

"I'll drive." Swede hooked her elbow and guided her to his truck, opened the door and handed her up.

He couldn't get over the transformation from the sweaty, dirt-covered ranch girl to the sexy redheaded temptress. His gaze swung her direction several times on the drive into Eagle Rock.

At least two dozen trucks lined the parking lot and the street around the Blue Moose Tavern. The thumps of drums and a bass guitar could be heard all the way out into the street even before Swede opened his door.

"I see Hank's truck," Allie said. "He and Sadie must already be inside." She waited for Swede to get out and come around to open her door. He reached in to capture her around the waist and helped her to the ground. He held on a moment or two longer than he should have, but he couldn't get his fingers to loosen their hold on her body.

"Ready to go?" she asked.

Oh, hell no. "Yes."

From the outside, the bar didn't look like much. Inside, it was a lot bigger than the exterior storefront indicated.

A three-man band played country-western music, and several couples were two-stepping their way around the dance floor.

"I see them." Allie grabbed his hand and led him, weaving between the tables, saying hello to almost everyone in the room. Several cowboys whistled when she walked by. One reached out to touch her leg, but a hard stare from Swede made him back off and turn his reach into a wave.

Hank and Sadie sat at a table facing the front entrance, with a broad-shouldered man seated in front of them with his back to the room.

Swede and Allie arrived at the table and the stranger turned and jumped to his feet, with a smile and a wince. "Swede. You son of a bitch. Good to see you." Bear, the Delta Force friend he'd made during rehab, pounded his back and hugged him so hard it hurt his ribs. The guy didn't know his own strength. The leg wound had done nothing to diminish his arm strength.

"And this must be your assignment." Bear winked. "Hi, Tate Parker. But call me Bear."

"Alyssa Patterson, but you can call me Allie." She shook his hand, but was pulled into a hug similar to the one Swede had endured.

Bear set her to arm's length and raked his gaze over her. "Allie, wearing a dress like that, you need to be on the dance floor. Care to dance with me?" He held out his arm. "I can't promise I won't step on your toes. The docs said I'd never dance again. But I fooled them. I never could dance, but what I lack in skill, I make up for in enthusiasm."

Allie laughed and followed Bear to the dance floor.

Swede stepped aside, wanting to punch his friend for taking off with his girl. Then he had to remind himself Allie wasn't his girl. In fact, she was Reynolds's girl, soon to be wife.

"What's wrong, Swede? You look like you swallowed a lemon." Hank nodded toward Bear. "I thought you would be happy to see your friend. He got in an hour ago and insisted on coming with us, even though he's been up since four this morning."

"Bear's a force to be reckoned with. I swear, he knows no limits to his physical abilities." Another glance Allie's way and Swede turned back to Hank. "I take it Bear will fit in with the team you're building?"

"Perfectly. I talked with him on the phone yesterday evening and had him on a plane first thing this morning."

"Great." Swede really was glad for the friend who'd been at his side through his own physical therapy and re-introduction into the civilian world. But did he have to hold Allie so close?

"I spoke with the fire chief. They found evidence of C-4 explosives and a detonator similar to the ones used by the military."

"Great. That tells me that whoever set that charge probably knew what he was doing."

Hank's lips firmed. "Afraid so."

Sadie leaned forward. "What I don't understand is how Damien could walk away from it all and leave his fiancée to answer to the sheriff and fire fighters." The pretty actress frowned. "If I were Allie, I'd dump his ass and call off the wedding."

"Before the explosions, he said he had a business emergency he had to deal with and the plane was waiting," Swede said. "But no business emergency is enough to leave the woman you love behind with the lingering threat of someone trying to blow you and her away."

Sadie smacked her palm on the table. "Damn right. I've got half a mind to tell her that."

Hank slipped his arm around Sadie. "That's what I like about you. Your passion." He kissed his wife. "Our baby is going to be hell on wheels when he's born."

Sadie lifted her chin. "She."

Swede smiled at the happy couple, glad his teammate had found the woman of his dreams. But they still had a big problem on their hands. One involving Hank's sister and her fiancé. "What do you know about Damien Reynolds, and any of the people who work for him?"

Hank retained his hold on his wife's hand, but he turned his attention back to the case. "I searched the web, looking for anything linked to Damien and found an article about him and his corporation being awarded a big government construction contract. I have a call in to a friend of mine who works in procurement in D.C. I'll let you know what I find."

Swede nodded toward Bear. "What have you got for Bear to work on?"

"I take it you haven't heard about the national guardsman who was attacked in Bozeman last night?"

Swede swung his gaze back to Hank. "No, I didn't. What happened?"

"I don't have all of the details. What I do know is that he was cut up pretty badly. Fortunately, someone found him shortly after the attack, and he was rushed to the hospital. Whoever did it sliced him open, basically eviscerating him."

Sadie gasped and covered her belly. "That's terrible!"

Swede's own gut clenched. "And he survived?"

"The guy who found him performed basic first aid, applying pressure to the wound. The first responders were able to get to him before he bled out, and the surgeon put his intestines back together. He's in ICU. He's not good, but they're hoping he makes it."

"Why would someone do that?" Sadie sat back in her chair, her face pale, her hand resting over her flat tummy.

"I don't know, but I'm putting Bear on it. The investigation doesn't pay, but the victim is a fellow serviceman. I feel we owe it to him to do something. He's a twenty-year-old kid, just back from deployment and only been home a day."

Swede's fists clenched. He wanted to kill the bastard who'd hurt the kid. He'd seen his share of stomach-turning atrocities, but that was in the Middle East where the Taliban and ISIS rebels had no regard for life. But this...Hell, they were on American soil with baseball and mom's apple pie. "Things like that shouldn't happen here," he said.

"Agreed."

"What do the Bozeman Police Department have to say about it?" Swede asked.

"They don't know what to think. As far as they could tell, they have no suspects, and they couldn't find a motivation for the attack. The guy's wallet was still on him, and he had five hundred dollars inside. For now, they're calling it a random act of violence."

"Bullshit." Swede's fists bunched. "It's just another way of saying they don't have a suspect or a clue as to who might have done it."

"Exactly. I want Bear to talk to the kid's family and his CO. I'm sure the police will be doing the same, but I won't feel right unless we do something to help find the bastard. In the meantime, you need to stick to Allie like glue. I don't think the two incidents are related, but I'd rather not take any chances. I love my little sister and don't want anything bad to happen."

"I'm on it." Swede pushed to his feet as the song ended. He crossed to the dance floor and tapped Bear's shoulder. "Mind if I cut in?"

Bear backed away, grinning. "Yes, I do mind, but I guess since it's you, I won't protest too much." He turned to Allie and raised her hand to press a kiss to the backs of her knuckles. "Thank you for the two-step lesson."

She nodded. "You're a quick study. Thank you for the dance."

Swede took her hand as the music transitioned into a slow, heart-breaking, belly-rubbing song.

Allie glanced up at him. "We can wait for a faster song, if you were hoping to two-step."

"No, this one is perfect." Perfect if she wasn't engaged to another man. Perfect to hold her close and sniff the strawberry scent of her hair. Perfect if she wasn't the body he was supposed to guard, and wasn't a woman getting married on Saturday.

ALLIE MELTED into Swede's arms, her body pressing close to his. She fit against him like they were made for each other. God, she had to stop thinking that way. On Saturday, she was supposed to marry the man of her dreams. What she was feeling was only pre-wedding jitters. Damien was the man for her, not Swede.

Then why was she leaning into his body, resting her cheek against his chest and wishing the song would never end?

With their hips touching, Allie knew immediately that she wasn't the only one feeling whatever it was building between them. The hard ridge of his fly pressed into her belly, the slow song lending itself to false dreams and dangerous passion.

As if of their own volition, her hands slipped up his chest and wrapped around the back of his neck.

Swede cupped her face, turning it up to his. "Do you know what you do to me?" he whispered.

"I have an idea," she said, her voice breathy. Allie couldn't seem to breathe normally. Not with Swede so close and the heat building between them.

His head dipped lower, and his lips hovered over

hers. If she leaned up on her toes, they'd kiss. It would be wrong. So very wrong. But…

As she bunched her muscles, she heard the music end, and the band announce a fifteen-minute break.

Swede straightened. "We should go back to the table."

"Yes, we should." Allie couldn't make her feet move.

"Look." Swede gripped her hands and squeezed hard. "Whatever this is, whatever we're feeling right now, isn't real."

Allie's chest tightened, and her eyes stung. "Of course, it isn't," she agreed, though her body felt otherwise.

"You're getting married on Saturday, and I'll move on to my next assignment. Let's not make this any harder than it has to be."

She nodded, knowing what he said couldn't be truer, even though she still wanted to feel his lips against hers. "You're right."

Swede stepped back, his arms falling to his sides.

Allie pasted a smile on her lips and forced air past her vocal cords. "Thank you for the dance. If you'll excuse me…" She made a beeline for the ladies' room. Once inside, she stood in front of the mirror, staring at the face of a woman who was engaged to one man and lusting after another. Her mother and father had raised her better than that. She ran cold water from the tap, stuck her hands beneath the spray and then splashed her cheeks with her wet hands.

"Hey." Sadie entered behind her and slipped an arm over Allie's shoulder. "Are you okay?"

Too disturbed to come up with a lie, she shook her head. "I don't know."

"You look a little flushed." Sadie ripped a paper towel from the roll, wet it and squeezed out the excess before patting Allie's face with it. "For a moment out there, I thought you and Swede were going to kiss."

Allie met Sadie's gaze in the mirror. "The bad part about it is that I wanted to," she admitted.

Sadie sighed. "Baby, are you sure Damien's the right man for you?"

Throwing her hands in the air, Allie spun and paced all three steps across the room and back. "I'm getting married on Saturday. No man I just met is going to derail my plans."

Sadie held up her hands. "Okay. You're getting married on Saturday." She tossed the wet paper towel in the trash and tore off a dry one. "If it's Damien you're determined to marry, then you have to stop drooling over your bodyguard."

Again, Allie's gaze met Sadie's in the mirror. Her shoulders slumped, and she nodded. "You're right. It's not right. I need to go home, get a good night's sleep and wake up with the right frame of mind."

"Don't forget, tomorrow we pick up your wedding dress," Sadie reminded her.

Allie's chest pinched. Instead of being giddy with excitement, like a bride should be, she dreaded going. She needed to call Damien. Maybe hearing his voice would help get her back on track. He was the man she was going to marry on Saturday. This was only a case of cold feet. Straightening her shoulders, she stepped out of the bathroom and ran into a wall of muscles.

Sadie squeezed by them and darted back into the bar room.

Some friend she was.

Swede's arms came up around her and crushed her against his chest. "Are you all right?"

"Yes." She nodded, and then shook her head. "No. I need to go home."

"We've only been here twenty minutes. Are you sure you don't want to stay and visit with your brother?"

"No. I'm tired and have a big day ahead of me." She stepped back. "If you want to stay, I can see if Bear will take me back to the ranch."

Swede's jaw hardened. "I'll take you." He hooked her elbow in a tight grip and led her back to the table where they said their goodbyes and then left the tavern.

Once outside, Allie sucked in deep breaths, hoping the fresh Montana air would clear her head.

Swede opened the truck door for her and handed her up into the passenger seat. The touch of his fingers against her elbow shot electric currents throughout her body and left her tingling. This couldn't be. Maybe she'd had too much to drink. Then she remembered, she hadn't had a chance to order a drink.

As she watched Swede walk around to the driver's side, Allie moaned softly. She needed to talk to Damien. What she was feeling was lonely and neglected. That was all.

Swede climbed into the driver's seat and shifted the truck in gear.

Allie stared out the side window, refusing to look his in direction. How he must be laughing at her, thinking she was a two-timing woman, eager to cheat on her fiancé while he was out of town. Allie wanted to tell him that wasn't the case. That she wasn't that kind of woman. But she'd had those feelings. And feeling it was almost as bad as actually doing it.

They'd driven past all the houses and continued onto the highway leading to the Bear Creek Ranch when headlights flashed brightly in the rearview mirror.

Swede squinted and tipped the windshield mirror upward. He decreased his speed a little, but the vehicle wasn't interested in passing.

Allie watched through the side mirror and finally turned in her seat to glance through the rear window. "What the hell is he trying to prove?"

Swede lowered his window and waved the guy on.

The headlights seemed to get larger as the vehicle sped up. Instead of swerving to go around, the SUV rammed into the back of the truck.

Allie jerked forward. The seatbelt snapped tight, keeping her from slamming into the dash.

"Hang on!" Swede yelled. "He's going to hit us again."

Allie braced her hand on the dash, her body already bruised from the first attack.

The trailing vehicle rammed them again, hitting at a bit of an angle.

Swede's truck fishtailed. He fought to straighten it before it ran off the road into a ditch. Just when he had it under control, the attacker raced up beside them and slammed into the driver's side.

The truck ran off the pavement onto the gravel shoulder.

Allie held onto the oh-shit handle above the door as Swede fought with the steering wheel to bring the truck back onto the blacktop.

It was hard to do with the attacking vehicle pushing him further off the road.

Swede changed tactics and slammed on his brakes. The truck skidded in the gravel but slowed faster than the attacking full-sized SUV. His maneuver bought them a few seconds, allowing Swede to drive back up onto the highway.

No sooner had he righted the truck, something hit the front windshield dead-center between the driver and passenger sides.

Allie's heart plunged into the pit of her belly. The hole in the windshield was perfectly round. "They're shooting at us!"

"Get down!" Swede shouted. He spun the steering wheel and hit the accelerator at the same time. The truck did a complete one-hundred-eighty-degree turn.

Another bullet blasted through the back windshield, through the headrest of the passenger seat and exited through the front windshield. If Allie hadn't ducked when Swede told her to, she would have been hit in the back of the head. Her stomach flipped, and she remained low in her seat.

"Switch places!" Swede yelled.

"What? Are you insane?"

"They're coming around. Hurry. Switch places." Swede shifted the seat back and slammed his foot on the accelerator.

Allie slid across the console and into Swede's lap. Once she had control of the steering wheel, he crawled out from under her and lifted his foot off the accelerator.

He fell across the other seat, righted himself, lowered the window and poked out his handgun.

The other vehicle had performed a slower version of the turnaround Swede had executed moments before and was now quickly catching up.

Her heart pounding against her ribs, Allie slammed her foot all the way down on the accelerator, while Swede leaned halfway out the window and fired.

The trailing SUV swerved, but kept coming.

Swede fired again, hitting one of the headlights.

Another bullet hit the back windshield, spraying glass fragments throughout the truck's interior.

Allie kept her head low and her gaze on the curving road ahead. Reaching town meant the guy behind them might veer off and leave them alone.

Swede fired again, but the SUV kept coming.

Allie rounded a curve, reaching out to grab Swede's belt to keep him from flying out.

He stayed with the truck and fired again on the SUV.

After flying around another curve and over a rise, Allie nearly cried out in relief when the lights of Eagle Rock twinkled from below. She drove faster, refusing to slow for the curves leading into town. The lights behind her disappeared as she made the last turn, drove onto

Main Street and straight toward the local sheriff's office.

Swede dropped back into the passenger seat, still holding his handgun in one hand, while his other covered his right shoulder.

Allie pulled into the parking lot of the county jail and sheriff's office, honking the truck's horn. She shoved the shift into park, dropped down out of the driver's seat and ran toward the door.

Sheriff Joe Barron stepped outside, his hand resting on the handle of his service weapon. "What the hell's going on?"

Allie stopped in front of him, breathing hard and shaking from head to toe. "Someone tried to kill us." She turned back to look at the road leading into town, happy to see it empty of traffic. Especially the kind of traffic that fires bullets.

Swede dropped down out of the truck, having holstered his handgun beneath his jacket. He held his hand over his right arm. "You don't happen to have a first aid kit in your office, do you?"

"I do."

"Good." Swede pulled his hand away from his arm. His palm and fingers were drenched, and the sleeve of his black leather jacket shone with wet, sticky blood.

Allie swayed, and her heart leaped into her throat. "Damn, Swede, you've been shot."

CHAPTER 6

WITHIN MINUTES, the volunteer firefighter paramedic, local doctor, Hank, Bear and Sadie converged on the sheriff's office. Between all of them, they insisted on moving Swede two buildings down to the only medical clinic in town.

Swede shook his head, insisting the injury was nothing but a flesh wound. Upon closer inspection, the doctor and paramedic agreed, but it had nicked him deep enough to cause a significant amount of bleeding.

"Did you get a look at the license plate?" Sheriff Barron asked.

Swede shook his head. "I didn't.'

"Me neither," Allie confirmed. "It all happened so fast, and bullets were flying. We didn't have time to breathe, much less jot down a license plate." She hovered near Swede, offering to hold the adhesive tape or hand them a bottle of rubbing alcohol when needed.

Swede let the doctor treat the wound. He'd seen

what happened when soldiers didn't take care of themselves. Infections could be lethal, or cause the loss of a limb. But he drew the line at stitches. "Just slap on a butterfly bandage. It'll heal."

The doctor flushed the wound with water and alcohol and then pressed a couple of bandages across it. "Change the bandage daily, or if it gets really dirty. Other than a nice scar, you'll probably live."

"Thought so."

"But not if that guy is still running loose." Allie held out Swede's jacket. Sadie had rinsed the blood out of it as best she could and dried it with towels and a blow dryer while the doc worked on him.

Sheriff Barron shook his head. "I don't know what's going on around here, but we have to get to the bottom of it. We can't have the good citizens of the county afraid to come outside."

"So far, Reynolds and Allie seem to be the targets," Hank said.

"Yeah. We're trying to track down the source of the C-4 and the paint used to deface the stable before it burned to the ground. The state forensics lab is working on it, and a hundred other hot cases." The sheriff drew in a deep breath and let it out. "In the meantime, to make sure you get home safe, I'll escort you to the Bear Creek Ranch, personally."

Allie smiled at her friend. "Thank you, Joe."

He draped an arm over her shoulders, and hugged her. "I'm sorry this is happening to you, but I'm glad you had someone like Mr. Svenson with you. Your own personal SEAL to keep you safe when the crap hits the fan."

Allie nodded, her gaze seeking and connecting with Swede's.

Swede felt a warmth flooding through him that had nothing to do with the jacket he'd shrugged into. The arm felt fine, but he'd like to get back to Bear Creek Ranch where Allie was surrounded by people who loved and looked out for her. After the attack that evening, Swede wasn't sure his skills were enough to keep Allie safe.

"You know, Allie," Sheriff Barron was saying. "You really might consider postponing your wedding. With the way things have been going, it would make too big a target for these yahoos to pass up."

Allie's eyes narrowed and her lips thinned. "I'm getting married on Saturday. Scare tactics aren't keeping me from my wedding."

The sheriff raised his hands. "Just saying, it might not be safe for you or your guests."

Her brows furrowing, Allie seemed to chew on Joe Barron's words. "I don't want anyone else to get hurt because of me." She looked up at her friend. "I'll think about it. But as far as anyone knows, the wedding is still on."

Swede's stomach bunched at the determination in Allie's voice. What did he expect? She was engaged to a wealthy man and had been, well before Swede showed up in Eagle Rock. Besides, he wasn't in the market for a long-term relationship. Not with his hang-ups. Hell, he was barely satisfactory at his new job. A man who was at one hundred percent would have taken out the attackers. But he'd missed, allowing the bastards to live.

Sheriff Barron waved toward the door. "Allie, if you're ready to go, I'll escort you two to the ranch gate."

Allie glanced at Swede.

Swede nodded. "We're ready."

"Call me when you get home." Hank pressed a kiss to Allie's forehead. "I like to know you're okay."

Sadie hugged her. "I'll see you tomorrow."

"Do you want us to swing by and pick you up for the trip into Bozeman?" Swede asked.

Hank shook his head. "No. We will all drive in at the same time. Sadie and I will meet you at the gate to the Bear Creek Ranch."

"And I'll bring up the rear," Bear said. "I want to swing by the hospital and check on the soldier, and then I'll go by his unit to talk to his commander."

Swede had wondered how it would be as a civilian, without the support and camaraderie of his SEAL team. Not much had changed. With Hank and Bear nearby, Swede knew they had his back. He hoped, between the three of them, they could keep Allie safe.

Allie insisted on driving Swede's truck back to the ranch. With the sheriff's SUV behind them, they had no repeat performances from the earlier attacker. The sheriff parked at the entrance to Bear Creek Ranch and waited until Allie was halfway to the house before he turned to go back to town.

"You have some good people here in Montana," Swede noted.

Allie snorted. "Except the ones trying to kill me?"

"With that exception. I think the good people outnumber the bad."

She nodded. "You're right. I love living here. I love the people I grew up with and the sense of community. Although, sometimes they can get into your business when you don't want them to. But for the most part, everyone looks out for everyone else."

"You're lucky to have them." Swede's hand rested on his pistol. Even though they were on the Bear Creek Ranch, he couldn't let down his guard for a moment. He had done so earlier, and it had almost gotten them killed. All because he'd wanted to kiss Allie.

And still did.

He sat in silence as Allie drove up to the house and parked.

"What will you tell my father about your truck?" Allie asked, staring at the holes in the windshield.

"I'll tell him I got behind a gravel truck."

"What about the dent in the door?"

"It could have been a rude driver in the Blue Moose parking lot, backing into me and driving off."

She nodded. "He might buy it."

"You need to talk to Damien," Swede said.

She stared at the house in front of her. "I know."

"He has to know more than he's telling us about this threat. If we could talk to him about it, we might have a better starting point in our search to locate the attacker."

"I'll try to get in touch with him tonight. If he's on the other side of the world, it might be difficult to contact him." Allie unbuckled her seatbelt and reached for the keys in the ignition.

"Why are you marrying Reynolds?" Swede asked before he could stop himself. It wasn't the kind of question a bodyguard asked his client. But there it was.

Her hand froze on the keys. "Why do you ask?" she countered. She didn't glance his way. Instead, she stared at the keyring.

Swede studied her face, looking for a reaction, a clue to her feelings about the man she had promised to marry. "I don't know him well, but you two just don't seem right for each other. Like you don't fit." Again, as soon as the words left his mouth, he wished he could have taken them back.

Allie's fingers curled around the keys, and her mouth pulled into a tight line. "You're right. You don't know Damien. And, for that matter, you don't know me." She pushed open the door, stepped down on the running board and dropped to the ground.

Swede rounded the front of the truck and took the keys she held out to him. "You didn't answer the question. Why are you marrying Damien?"

Allie pushed back her shoulders and met his gaze. "That's none of your business. You're just the bodyguard my fiancé hired to protect me. After the wedding, I'll be on my way to the Cayman Islands, and you'll be on to your next assignment. What does it matter?"

Swede gripped her arms, wanting to wring the truth out of the woman. But, he knew she was right. It wasn't his business. Still, he didn't understand the relationship between Allie and Damien, and one thing was bugging the hell out of him. "You never said you loved him."

Allie stared up into his eyes, her hands pressed to his chest, neither pushing him away nor bringing him closer. "I don't have to say the words to you."

Swede pulled her closer until their bodies touched, hip to hip, breasts to chest. "Do you want to kiss him when you're dancing?"

"Why are you doing this?" she whispered. "You said you aren't into relationships. Why are you interested in mine?"

"Answer my question." He leaned closer, his mouth moving nearer to hers.

Allie licked her lips, sending a burst of flame through Swede's system. He couldn't go back now that he'd started down this path.

Swede's voice dropped lower, his groin tightening as the ridge beneath his fly rubbed against Allie's belly. "Does he make you want to fall into bed and make love to him with only a glance?"

"You don't know what you're doing," she said, her gaze slipping to his mouth, her tongue sweeping across her lips again.

"*Me?* I think *you* don't know what you're doing. Or what you really want."

"And you know me well enough to know what I want and need?" she challenged.

"No, but I know what *I* want." His hands slipped down her arms and around to rest on her lower back. "I want that kiss." Then Swede broke all the rules he associated with being a bodyguard and kissed the woman he was sworn to protect. Not only did he kiss her, he branded her with his mouth, taking everything she would give and sweeping past her teeth to take even more.

Their tongues danced a sensual tango, thrusting and parrying.

Allie's hands slid beneath Swede's jacket, curled over his chest and locked behind his neck, pulling him closer.

Swede knew what he was doing was wrong, but something drew him to Allie. Something he found irresistible. Unfortunately, one kiss would never be enough. With her imminent marriage to a man who didn't care enough about his fiancée to be with her when someone was out to kill her, looming, Swede's stomach knotted and his heart hurt. He tore his lips away from hers.

"No." Swede lifted his head and stared down into her face. "No."

Allie looked up into his eyes, her green ones glazed, her breathing coming in labored breaths. Her body still pressed to his, her hands flattened against his chest. She blinked and the glaze cleared. Her eyes widened, and she gasped. "Damn you." Allie stepped back and swung her arm, her palm connecting with his face in a resounding slap.

Swede's cheek stung with the force of the blow. He stood there, unmoving, knowing he deserved every bit of it. "I'm sorry. I shouldn't have done that."

Through gritted teeth, she said, "Don't. Ever. Touch. Me. Again." She spun on her heels and ran in the house.

If he wasn't mistaken, Swede could swear he heard a sob before the door closed behind Allie.

SHE DIDN'T STOP RUNNING until she reached the sanctuary of her bedroom. After she shut the door, Allie leaned her back against it and slid to the floor. Tears rolled down her cheeks. Allie touched her fingers to the tears. What was wrong with her? She was never this emotional. The last time she cried was the day her mother died. Since then, her father insisted crying was only for babies. She wasn't a baby; she was a grown woman with a wedding ahead of her.

For a minute more, she allowed herself to sink into the depths of despair, sobbing quietly so that her bodyguard couldn't hear her break down. Then she got up, stripped out of the pretty dress, wadded it into a ball and stuffed it in the very back of her closet. If she never wore the dress again, that was just fine with her.

Pulling a T-shirt over her head, Allie peeked out into the hallway. Nothing moved. A light shined beneath the door of Hank's old bedroom, her father's room was dark and the bathroom door across the hall was open with the light on. She crossed to the bathroom, closed and locked the door, then brushed her teeth and scrubbed off the little bit of makeup that hadn't washed away with her tears.

Allie brushed her hair and secured it in a ponytail on top of her head. Looking in the mirror, she appeared much like the little girl who'd lost her mother. Right now she missed her mom more than ever. When she opened the door, she half-feared, half-wished she'd run into Swede in the hallway. Again, it was empty.

After trudging across the corridor to her room, she closed the door and collapsed on the bed. She lifted the phone, dialed Damien's number and waited. She heard one ring and his phone rolled over to voicemail.

Damn.

Tomorrow she really needed to talk to Damien. That kiss had only made matters worse. Now, not only had she cheated in thought, she'd cheated in deed. How could she go into a marriage with the guilt of that kiss weighing on her mind? Then again, how could she tell Damien without hurting him?

Allie curled up on the bed, hugging a pillow to her chest. For a long time, she lay still, willing herself to sleep, hoping everything would appear brighter with the morning sunshine.

After tossing and turning until the wee hours of the morning, Allie finally drifted to sleep.

It was her wedding day. She wore the dress she had picked out, and had her hair piled high on her head with ringlets falling down her back. Her father walked her down the aisle very slowly, his face grim. As they passed the rows of guests, people whispered and pointed. They knew. Her face heated and her belly churned.

When Allie finally reached the altar, she turned to face the man who would become her husband until death should they part. But Damien wasn't the one waiting for her. The man in the tuxedo stood taller and straighter. A man of military bearing and discipline. Waiting to marry her was the man who'd been hired by her fiancé to protect her.

Swede.

Pounding on her door woke her at 8:00 the next

morning. Her father's voice boomed through the paneling. "If you want to eat, you need to come down, now. Georgia is cleaning the kitchen, and she's waiting on you."

"I'm coming," Allie responded. One glance at the clock made her throw back the comforter and leap out of the bed. "Why didn't anyone wake me earlier?"

"Swede said you didn't get to bed until late. We decided you needed your beauty sleep."

Allie crossed the room to her dresser and selected a pullover blouse. "Are you saying I'm looking more like a hag lately?" She ripped her sleep shirt over her head, put on a bra and dragged on the clean shirt she'd wear to town.

"I wouldn't say that," her father said. "But you have had dark circles beneath your eyes. I think you work too hard."

Allie stuck her feet into her jeans and pulled them up, securing the zipper. "Well, that plays right into my plans for today. I'm going to Bozeman to pick up my wedding dress. That means I won't be around to help out in the hay field until late this evening." She grabbed a pair of walking shoes and the high heels she'd wear under her wedding dress and opened her bedroom door.

"The hay won't be dry enough to bale until tomorrow. Take your time."

"Thanks, Dad." She glanced at her father, sensing he wanted to say more, but couldn't come up with the words to express the emotions playing across his face. Well, as much emotion as Lloyd Patterson ever expressed. The man was taciturn and rough around the edges, but Allie knew deep down he loved her and Hank, and only wanted the best for them.

Her father stared at her for a moment longer. "I heard what happened last night."

Allie's fists clenched. She shouldn't have slapped Swede for kissing her, and she sure as hell shouldn't have kissed him in the first place. Today, after she picked up her wedding dress, she'd call Damien and confess that she was confused and scared and…well… she'd come up with a good reason for kissing her body-guard. Although, she couldn't at the moment, other than she'd wanted to more than she wanted to breathe. "Look, Dad, what happened last night won't happen again."

His brows furrowed. "How do you know it won't happen again?"

She squared her shoulders. "Because I'm not going to let it."

Her father shook his head, his gaze narrowing to a slit. "I don't see how you can keep it from happening again until they catch the guy who did it. From what Sheriff Barron said, you didn't even get a look at the license plate. How will they find the shooter if you didn't even get that?"

Allie almost laughed out loud at her father's words. Holy hell, she'd thought he was talking about the kiss. Thank goodness the people who knew about that would remain the only two. Until she confessed to her fiancé. *If* she confessed. "You're right, Dad. It could happen again. We just have to hope it doesn't."

"I'm just glad your friend Swede was with you. I can't imagine what would have happened had you been alone." He took her hands. "With the wedding so close, and this shooter still on the loose, don't you think you should consider postponing?"

What was with everyone trying to convince her to postpone or call off her wedding? "It was probably a random act. I'm getting married on Saturday. I've spent too much money on everything, and it's non-refundable."

"That's no reason to get married. Here you are in trouble, and your fiancé isn't anywhere around to keep you safe." Her father dropped her hands, a scowl making deep grooves in his forehead. "What kind of man doesn't take care of his woman?"

"He'll be back before the wedding. You can ask him then." Allie stepped past her father. "In the meantime, I have a wedding dress to pick up at the bridal shop."

"I really wish you'd stay here at the ranch. I don't want to see you hurt."

"I'll have Sadie, Hank and Swede with me. If I need help, they have offered to provide it." She didn't wait around to argue further. Allie hurried down to the kitchen.

"You'll have to hustle if you want breakfast before you leave for your appointment at the dressmakers." Georgia held out a plate of fluffy scrambled eggs. "Hank called. He and Sadie will be at the gate in ten minutes."

"I'm not hungry. But thanks." Allie aimed straight for the coffee pot, poured half a cup and downed it, burning her tongue. With her father's words and the images of her dream still rattling around in her head, Allie braced herself and stepped out on the porch.

Swede sat on the porch steps, scratching Ruger behind the ears. When he heard the door open, he stood and faced her. "I've been thinking."

Allie marched down the steps and out to her truck, her keys in hand. "That's nice."

"What happened last night—"

"It didn't." Allie turned to face him. "Nothing happened last night. Get it?"

Swede pressed his hand to the cheek Allie had slapped the night before. "Sure felt like it happened."

"Don't ever let it happen again."

"I wasn't the only one kissing." He grabbed her arm and forced her to stop and look at him. "You weren't fighting me."

Allie glared and looked back at the house. "Shh. Whatever happened cannot happen again. On either side."

"Trust me. I won't kiss you again." He let go of her arm, walked to her truck and stopped next to the passenger side. "Not unless you ask me." His lips twitched on the corners.

Allie contemplated hurling her keys at him. How dare he laugh at such a huge mistake? She refused to rise to his bait. Instead, she climbed into the driver's seat, fit the key into the ignition and started the engine.

Swede tried the handle on the passenger side. "Hey, unlock the door."

For a moment, Allie considered driving off without the infuriating man. One glance at the bullet holes in his truck changed her mind. She popped the locks and waited for him to climb in.

"I thought you were going to leave without me."

"Believe me, I almost did." She slammed the gear into reverse, backed up and turned around, heading for the gate.

As agreed upon, Sadie and Hank were waiting in Hank's pickup. Bear, in one of Hank's White Oak Ranch trucks, waited behind them.

Allie waved as she passed the two trucks and drove all the way into Bozeman without saying another word to Swede.

"Stop at the hospital. Hank, Bear and I want to talk to the kid who got cut up."

With a nod, no words, Allie turned and headed for the hospital, pulling into a visitors' slot.

Allie turned off the engine but made no move to get out. "I'll wait out here."

Swede was halfway out of the truck. "Like hell, you will." He rounded to the other side and grabbed her door handle.

Moving quickly, she hit the door lock. Her gaze went from the lock to his eyes.

Swede frowned and tried the door handle. "Allie, don't be ridiculous. You can't stay out here by yourself. Please, unlock the door."

She stared at him for a long moment and then sighed. Who was she kidding? She might as well paint a big red bulls-eye on her and the truck.

She tapped the button releasing the locks and slid out of the truck.

CHAPTER 7

Swede let out a long breath and touched her arm. "I'm sorry for anything I've said or done that makes you not want me to protect you. I promise not to touch you or make you uncomfortable. But please, don't lock me out."

Allie shook her head. "No, that was childish of me. I won't do it again." She held up her hand. "I promise."

The other two trucks pulled in and parked nearby. Sadie joined Allie and took her hand. The men surrounded the women as they entered the hospital.

At the information desk, Bear asked for Thomas Baker, the soldier brought in with knife wounds.

The volunteer keyed something into the computer and waited a moment. Then she looked up and smiled. "He's in ICU."

"How is he?" Bear asked.

The gray-haired lady shrugged. "You'll have to speak with the nurses in ICU. They'll be able to tell you more."

They rode the elevator up to ICU.

Nurses hurried from room to room, tending to seriously ill patients, taking vital signs, administering medication and trying to make their patients more comfortable in an uncomfortable situation.

Hank approached the nurses' station and asked to see Thomas Baker.

"Are you a relative of Mr. Baker?" the head nurse asked.

"No," Hank responded. "I'm a war veteran, come to pay my respects to the young soldier. He deserves a whole lot more than what he got from the low-life who did this."

The nurse nodded. "Agreed. But rules are rules. Only relatives are allowed into the room. Unless Mr. Baker requests to see you."

"We'd like to talk to him about the attack, in case there is anything we can do to help, or keep this from happening to others."

"Isn't that what the police are doing?" asked the head nurse. "They were in an hour ago, after Mr. Baker woke."

"I imagine they are doing a fine job of finding the attacker," Hank said. "But we'd still like to help."

The woman behind the counter stared at Hank for a long moment and finally said, "Get the family's permission to visit with Mr. Baker, and I'll bend the rules for you this once." Her eyes narrowed. "But, if you do anything to upset my patient, you'll be thrown out of here so fast you won't know what hit you."

Hank held up both hands. "We're here to help, not hurt."

"His mother and father are in the ICU waiting room. You can catch up with them there. They must agree or you're not getting in to see the young man."

"We understand," Bear assured her.

As they walked away from the nurses' station, Allie asked, "What if you can't get in to see Baker?"

"Bear will be making an appointment to visit with the soldier's commander," Hank said. "Maybe he can shed light on what happened."

In the ICU waiting room, the only other people present were a man and a woman appearing tense and exhausted.

Hank stopped just inside the door. "The rest of you should find a seat. I'd like to talk to Baker's parents with just me and Bear, so as not to overwhelm them."

"Right." Swede followed Allie to a seat on the far side of the waiting room. He sat on one side, and Sadie sat on the other.

A few minutes later, Hank, Bear and Baker's parents left the waiting room.

Swede wished he could be a fly on the wall in Thomas Baker's room, but he was content to be next to Allie. With all of the attacks on her and then this one on Baker, he wasn't comfortable leaving her alone here in the hospital. Forget about leaving her out in the parking lot.

Allie turned to Sadie. "Have you had any morning sickness, yet?"

Sadie shrugged. "A little, but nothing unmanageable. I still can't believe we're having a baby in seven months."

Allie grinned. "I can't wait. Hank's going to make a

great father. And I'm over-the-moon about being an aunt."

Swede listened to the ladies talking, a little envious of Hank. The man had a family and a baby on the way. Wow. Nothing could be more grounding than having a child and a wife. A glance at Allie made him wonder what it would be like to be married to a woman like her, and to have children. He could picture an auburn-haired little girl running through the yard, her curls bouncing on her shoulders. She'd laugh and play with her mother, beautiful and carefree.

Too bad that child wouldn't be his. That thought caught him by surprise. He'd never considered himself good husband material, especially after all the operations he'd been on. Shooting other people and being shot at did something to a man. As if the nightmares, ducking at every loud noise, always easing around corners and looking behind you for the enemy weren't enough, trying to fit into a society at once familiar and yet foreign was a challenge in itself. Most people Stateside were only worried about what they were cooking for dinner, not whether they would live to see their next meal.

Like so many other combat veterans, Swede found the transition hard and didn't wish his problems on anyone. Especially an attractive, independent woman like Allie.

Sitting with Allie and Sadie, hearing talk of renovating a room for the baby reminded Swede that his buddy Hank was getting on with his life. He'd been through everything Swede had, and more. If he could move on and give himself a chance at a real life with a family and children, why couldn't Swede?

He glanced at Allie.

Reynolds didn't know how good he had it. His fiancée was amazing. She'd make a great aunt, and an even better mother.

Hank and Bear entered the waiting room five minutes later, their faces grim.

Swede stood. "What did you learn?"

"Baker is lucky to be alive," Bear said.

Hank pushed a hand through his hair. "From what his parents and the nurse said, his attacker gutted him and left him to die."

"Was he able to give a description of the attacker, or any kind of motivation?" Swede asked.

"No," Hank said.

"He wasn't involved with a girl, so no ex-boyfriend issues." Bear's jaw tightened. "The kid was jumped walking home from getting a lousy hamburger yesterday evening. He didn't provoke anyone or start a fight. Hell, he'd barely said two words to the server at the hamburger joint."

"Bear is headed to Baker's unit," Hank said. "Since it wasn't a robbery, and he just returned from a deployment, maybe his commander can tell us whether or not he'd had any troubles with other unit members."

"I'll be with the ladies all afternoon." Swede nodded toward Hank and Bear. "Let us know what you find out."

"Will do." Hank glanced at Allie and Sadie. "You two stay close to Swede. If there's a nutcase walking around stabbing people, we don't want him taking a crack at you."

Sadie and Allie stood and edged a little closer to Swede.

"We'll stay with him," Sadie said, giving Swede a sad look. "Poor guy. He'll have to put up with sitting in a bridal shop while we try on our dresses."

"I can handle it," Swede said. Better to suffer through a female shopping trip than to worry whether or not they'd make it home alive.

Bear smirked. "Better you than me, buddy." He winked at the women. "Not that spending an afternoon with two beautiful women sounds bad at all, it's just all that talk about fabric and lace makes me itch."

"Same here," Hank agreed.

Sadie pointed toward the exit. "We could do without your negativity. The final fitting of the bride's gown is supposed to be a happy, optimistic time. We're better off without the two of you."

She hooked Swede's arm. "Come on, Swede, we'll have a nice afternoon, despite those two."

Hank snagged Sadie around the waist and hugged her to him. "Kiss me, you ornery woman, before I turn you over my knee and spank you."

She laughed up at him. "Not in front of the others." And she kissed him, long and hard, melting into his body.

Swede shifted uncomfortably, bumping into Allie.

"Disgustingly mushy, if you ask me," Allie whispered.

"I heard that," Sadie said, breaking off the kiss.

They walked to the elevator together, returned to the ground floor and exited the hospital.

Hank left in Bear's truck. "I'll have him drop me off at the bridal store when we're done poking around."

Sadie drove Hank's truck while Allie and Swede rode together the few blocks to the bridal shop.

Inside the building, the attendant hustled Sadie and Allie to the dressing rooms. Another attendant showed Swede to a cushioned seat to wait. Around him were full-length mirrors and more seats. He chuckled quietly. If his SEAL teammates could see him now, they'd howl with laughter. Badass SEAL surrounded by tulle and taffeta, or whatever it was they made wedding dresses out of.

Sadie was first to emerge from the dressing room in a pretty sky-blue dress. She lifted her skirt and walked toward Swede. "What do you think?"

He shrugged. "It's nice."

"Allie wanted sky-blue to remind her of the Montana skies. I like the sentiment." She turned away and stared at herself in the mirror. "Although, it's a good thing she's getting married Saturday. I don't know how much longer I'll fit in this dress." She ran her hands over her belly. "It won't be long before I start showing." She smiled, her eyes glazing with tears. "I'm going to be a mommy. And Hank's going to be a father." Sadie glanced at Swede in the mirror. "It's a big change from fighting the Taliban and ISIS, huh?"

Swede nodded.

"Ta, da!" The attendant who'd disappeared with Allie

opened the dressing room door and stepped aside with a flourish. "And we have the bride. Isn't she beautiful?"

Allie stepped out of the dressing room, her cheeks a rosy red, her gaze locked on Sadie.

"Oh, Allie." Sadie clapped her hands together. "You look amazing."

Swede swallowed hard past the constriction in his throat.

Allie, the cowgirl who could ride like she was born in a saddle, who loved ranch life and getting her hands dirty, had transformed from girl next door to...Oh, hell, a radiant and beautiful princess in a lacy white dress that hugged her body from the strapless neckline all the way down past her hips where it flared out, ending in a long train. The attendant had swept up her hair on her head and fixed it with a pearl comb.

Allie's gaze shifted from Sadie to Swede. She didn't say anything.

Swede could only stare. This woman was preparing to marry another man. How could he comment when all he wanted to do was say *No! Don't marry Reynolds! He doesn't deserve you.*

To keep from uttering those words, Swede had to get outside. Fast. He pushed to his feet and walked out of the viewing room, out of the building and into the fresh Montana air. There he sucked in a long, steadying breath. Then another. No matter how many breaths he took, he couldn't seem to get enough air into his lungs to ease the pressure.

One thing became very clear to him. He didn't want

the bride he was sworn to protect and get to the church on time to marry Damien Reynolds.

"WHAT THE HELL JUST HAPPENED?" Allie stood with her hands on her lace-covered hips, staring at the empty doorframe Swede had just passed through.

"He's a man. They can't handle all this girl stuff." Sadie tilted her head to the side and tapped her chin. "Or, is it that he didn't like seeing you in a dress you'd be wearing to marry another man?"

"Don't be ridiculous." Allie turned her back to Sadie. "Unzip me. The dress is fine. We can leave as soon as you're ready." She couldn't wait to get out of the dress shop. Really, she couldn't wait to ask Swede why he'd run out like a cat with his tail on fire.

"What's up between you and Swede?" Sadie asked.

"Nothing," Allie replied, a little too quickly. She took a deep breath and answered more slowly. "Nothing. I'm marrying Damien on Saturday." *Come hell or high water.*

"Look, Allie, you don't have to go through with this wedding."

"I accepted his proposal. I'm marrying Damien on Saturday." She refused to be a wishy-washy bride. Having made her decision, she should stick to it.

Sadie finished unzipping the back of the dress and turned Allie to face her. "You don't have to marry him."

"I keep my word."

"This is a case where you can break your promise, if it doesn't feel right." Sadie squeezed her hands. "From the look on your face, it doesn't feel right, does it?"

"I don't know." Holding the front of the dress up, Allie turned to the mirror, trying to see what Sadie saw in her face. But all she saw was a cheater who'd kissed her bodyguard. "I need to see Damien. Everything will be okay once he's back in town."

"Will it?" Sadie rested her hands on Allie's shoulders.

"This is all pre-wedding jitters. I'll be fine as soon as Damien is back in town."

Sadie planted her hands on her hips and stared at Allie in the mirror. "Okay, assuming you really love Damien, and you still want to marry him, tell me why. What's so great about him that you can't see yourself with any other man?"

That was the problem, Allie *could* see herself with another man. *Swede.* Hell, he'd been the groom in her wedding dream. What was the matter with her? Damien was everything a woman could want in a husband. "He's handsome," Allie started. In a preppy, businessman way. Not in that rugged, outdoorsy way, like Swede.

Not helping.

"So? Handsome isn't everything. I work around extremely handsome men in Hollywood." Sadie snorted. "Trust me, handsome isn't everything."

"He's a very successful businessman," Allie stated.

"So, he knows how to make money. How important is that to you? You and your father haven't wanted for anything. What can money buy that you don't already have?"

"I can travel more. See the world." *Damn was she that materialistic?*

"With a man you're not sure you're in love with?"

Sadie crossed her arms over her chest. "I'd rather stay home. I've been on sets in different countries. Without someone you love to share the excitement of exploring a foreign country, the trip is just sad and lonely."

"Damien's a fine horseman. Swede never rode a horse until he came to Bear Creek Ranch."

Sadie's eyes widened, and she pointed a finger at Allie. "Ah ha! You're comparing Damien to Swede. You *do* feel something there, or you wouldn't."

"I don't feel anything where Swede is concerned." Allie hiked up her skirt with one hand and marched into the dressing room, slamming the door. "You're reading way too much into my relationship with my bodyguard. He's just the hired help. Nothing more. He said so himself."

"But you wish it was more, don't you?" Sadie's voice was soft, barely audible through the door.

Allie let the dress fall to the floor like her heart sinking into her gut. *No.* She didn't wish Swede could be more than the hired help. It would mess up everything. "I'm marrying Damien."

"Allie, the big question is, do you love him?" Sadie said through the door.

Her chest tightened, and her throat constricted. Did she love Damien? Or had she been in love with the idea of getting married? "I'm not getting any younger," she whispered.

"You're only twenty-seven. You have years of dating and meeting more men in front of you."

"I know all the men in Eagle Rock and the surrounding ranches. I don't want any of them."

"Do you want Damien because he's not from Eagle Rock, or because you love him?"

God, why was Sadie pushing her into saying something she didn't want to say? Allie leaned against the door, tears filling her eyes. "Please, Sadie, stop."

For a long moment, silence reigned.

"I'm sorry, Allie. I won't say anything else other than I love you like the sister I never had. I don't want to see you marry someone you don't love. Marriage is hard, even when you *do* love your spouse. It's harder when you have nothing in common, and you don't love one another." She paused. "I'm going to be a mother. I can't imagine letting a child of mine enter a loveless marriage. That would be so unfair to him or her. Think about it, Allie."

Allie stepped out of the dress as several warm tears slipped from the corners of her eyes and rolled down her cold cheeks. She dressed quickly, left the room and handed the wedding gown to the attendant who'd stood patiently and discreetly out of the way during the whole conversation.

"Will you be taking the dress, today?" she asked.

"Yes." Allie didn't want to make another trip to town for it.

Sadie hugged her. "Ready to go home? I'm sorry if I upset you."

Allie shrugged. "I'm okay. I need to get a good night's sleep. We're hauling hay tomorrow."

"Seriously?" Sadie shook her head. "Your wedding, should you choose to go through with it, is in a couple of days."

"Wedding or not, the hay has to be baled and loaded into the barn." The hard work and long day would keep her occupied so much that she wouldn't have time to think. If she was going through with the wedding, the chores had to be done before the big day.

If.

Damn. Now she was thinking *if*, not *when*.

CHAPTER 8

SWEDE HELD the door for Allie as she hung the wedding dress in the back seat of the truck and then climbed into the passenger seat. The ride home from the bridal shop was uneventful, and completely and painfully silent.

Hank and Bear had returned from their visit to Baker's unit, arriving as Swede and the ladies left the bridal shop. The commander wasn't in, having gone to Wyoming earlier that morning. They expected him to be back the next day.

Bear had stayed in Bozeman to run by the police station and see if he could get any information from them about the stabbing. Hank and Sadie followed Swede and Allie to the gate of Bear Creek Ranch. As they pulled off the road at the entrance, Hank waved at Allie. "I can be by in the morning to help with the hay."

"Thanks. I'm sure Dad and Eddy can use all the help they can get," Allie said.

When they left, Swede turned to Allie. "I take it we're

hauling hay tomorrow?" He didn't like that he'd been left out of the conversation until now.

"You don't have to. It's not part of the job description."

"If you're out hauling hay, I'm out hauling hay."

Allie opened her mouth for a moment and then snapped it shut.

Dinner was much the same. Mr. Patterson and Eddy talked about baling and loading the hay the next day.

Swede wasn't clear on all the terms they used. He nodded when he thought he should.

"Allie, are you driving the truck for us? Or should I get Georgia to drive?" Eddy asked.

"Since Swede will be here, why not let him drive? I can help load the hay," Allie suggested.

Georgia's brows furrowed. "Don't be silly. Your wedding is in a couple days, you can't go out and get scratched and bruised. You want to have perfect skin and no sunburn for the big day. I'll drive the truck, and you'll stay at the house and cook dinner."

"No, ma'am." Allie said. "I want to help with the hay, and you know I can't boil eggs without burning the water."

"Then you'll drive, and Swede can help load," her father said. "Since that's settled, why don't you get some sleep? We have to be up by dawn to get this cutting done in a day."

"But—"

"No buts. Go to bed." Her father left the table and climbed the stairs.

"You'd think I was a little girl," Allie mumbled. "I'm a

grown woman, with a mind of my own," she said louder. "I don't need my daddy telling me when to go to bed."

"I heard that," her father said.

Swede's lips twitched, but he fought the smile.

Allie stared at him through narrowed eyes. "Don't laugh. It only encourages him."

Unable to hold back, Swede laughed out loud.

Eddy clapped a hand on his back. "She's as stubborn as her father."

Allie glared at Eddy. "I'm in the room."

Georgia patted her back. "Yes, dear, you are. Now, go to bed. Maybe a good night's sleep will improve your disposition."

"My disposition is just fine, thank you very much." But she rose from her chair, carried her plate to the sink and climbed the stairs to her room.

Swede waited thirty minutes before going to bed, giving Allie enough time to get through the shower and back to her room. He didn't want to bump into her in the hallway. He was afraid he'd try to kiss her again. And that wouldn't do.

SLEEP WAS A LONG TIME COMING, and dawn arrived too soon.

The sound of boots on the stairs woke him. He hurried to dress and get downstairs before the others left without him.

Lloyd and Eddy were just finishing breakfast when Swede walked into the kitchen.

"You two can join us at the barn when you're done here," Mr. Patterson said. "We have to connect the trailer and fuel the tractor."

"I won't be long," Swede promised.

Georgia set a heaping plate of food in front of him.

He stared down at it. "Looks good, ma'am, but I can't eat all of that."

She laughed. "You'll burn it off before noon. Eat."

Allie entered, dressed in jeans, a long-sleeved shirt, boots and a cowboy hat. She tossed another cowboy hat on the table next to Swede. "That's one of Hank's old hats. You'll need it today. Try it."

Swede settled the hat on his head. It fit perfectly.

Allie sat across from him, but never lifted her head to look him in the eye.

Georgia kept up a running commentary about some of the local gossip, seemingly unaware of the tension between Swede and Allie.

By the time Swede choked down half of the food Georgia insisted he eat, he'd had enough. He pushed back from the table, lifted his plate and carried it to the counter. "Please cover that, and I'll eat the rest for dinner tonight."

"Are you sure?" she asked.

"Positive." He kissed the older woman's cheek. "Thank you for all you do."

Georgia blushed and waved a hand at him. "Get out of here. You'll have Eddy jealous if he catches you kissing me."

Allie stood as well and carried her plate to the sink. "Thank you, Georgia."

"I'll bring sandwiches for lunch," Georgia promised.

Swede walked out of the house first and scanned the vicinity, not expecting trouble, but keeping aware was an essential part of his job. They hadn't expected trouble at Reynolds's stable, and it had exploded in their faces.

Hank arrived as Swede and Allie joined Eddy and Mr. Patterson at the barn. Eddy would bale the hay while the other men loaded the bales on the trailer.

Allie drove the truck through the hayfield, inching along at a snail's pace. Ruger walked along beside the truck, occasionally chasing a rabbit or digging for a prairie dog.

Swede considered himself in pretty good shape since rehab, but the work was hard, the hay was itchy, and the sun beat down on them throughout the day. By noon, Swede and Hank had shed their shirts, their bodies covered in sweat and hay dust.

"It's been a while since I've hauled hay," Hank said. "Now I remember why I disliked it." He ran his hand through his hair, loosening the stray straws. "But, you always feel good about what you accomplish when all the bales are neatly stacked in the barn."

Swede tossed another bale on top of the ever-increasing stack. Hank's father manned the top of the pile, stacking the bales in an overlapping pattern to keep them from falling off. "It's good, hard work." And it helped him keep his mind off Allie. Except she was driving the truck. Every time he glanced up, he could see her face in the side mirror.

As her bodyguard, it was hard not to focus on her.

Even out in the hayfield, he had to be on his toes. Whoever shot at them from the vehicle the other night, could be hiding at the edge of the pasture with a high-powered sniper rifle.

Swede glanced around again, his gaze coming back to Allie in the mirror.

"Did Bear hear anything new from the police?" Swede asked. Anything to take his thoughts off Allie.

"Nothing we didn't already know from talking to Baker and his parents." Hank tossed a bale up onto the back of the trailer. "Bear would have come to help here, but he's headed to Baker's unit to wait for the commander to return from Wyoming."

"I'd like to get my hands around the throat of the guy who attacked the kid."

"You and me both." Hank wiped the sweat from his brow and walked to the next bale in the field. "It's bugging the crap out of me that I can't come up with a single motivation for the attack."

"It's some crazy son-of-a-bitch who happened by at the same time Baker felt like having a hamburger."

Hank shook his head. "My gut tells me the attack is more than that."

"I'd like to help with the investigation," Swede said.

"You are, by keeping an eye on my little sister. She's got enough problems." Hank shot a glance toward Allie. "I tried to call Reynolds last night. He didn't pick up. I left a message, but he didn't get back to me."

"Allie doesn't even know where he went on his business trip," Swede said. "What kind of guy leaves his fiancée a few days before his wedding and doesn't share where he's going?"

"Maybe he's having an illicit affair with one of his clients." Hank's jaw tightened. "In which case, I'll have to kill him for hurting my sister."

"Get in line." Swede's fists clenched. He flexed his injured hand, the ache building with each bale. But he didn't stop to cry about it. The ache reminded him to keep focused on what had to be done.

Protect Allie.

"Has Allie said anything about what she'll do if her fiancé doesn't show up for the wedding?"

"Not at all. She keeps repeating that she's getting married Saturday." Swede chuckled. "I believe if Reynolds doesn't show up for his wedding, she'll kill him."

Hank laughed out loud. "Sounds like Allie. She's a very determined and stubborn woman. She gets it from our father."

"What does she see in Reynolds?"

"I haven't a clue, and I really don't know him well enough to judge him. Except that he's not here when shit's hitting the fan with my sister. That's a really big strike in my book." Hank glanced up at his father on top of the stack of hay. "Does my father know why you're here?" he said in a lowered voice.

Swede shook his head. "Allie insisted on calling me a friend from college, here for her wedding. Mrs. Edwards knows."

"It's probably just as well. My father might go off half-cocked with both barrels loaded, looking for the crackpot taking shots at his little girl. And I don't think he approves of this marriage."

"Does anyone, except Allie?" Swede chose that moment to glance at the mirror.

Allie was staring back at him, her eyes narrowed. Had she heard him mention her name?

Swede switched sides of the truck. Seeing Allie in the mirror only made him want to shake her. Why was she insisting on marrying a man who clearly didn't care enough about her to be there when she was in trouble? Trouble that could have been brought on by his own business dealings, and her association with him.

When Reynolds returned from his business trip, Swede wanted to have a few words with the man.

THE DAY CRAWLED by at the pace Allie drove the pickup pulling the hay trailer. She counted the minutes until all of the hay was loaded into the barn. Then, and only then, could she get away from the sight of a shirtless Swede, muscles bulging with the weight of the bales as he tossed them like toys into the air. Every time she glanced into the side-view mirror, he was there, looking back at her. How was she supposed to quit thinking about him when he was larger than life and freakin' gorgeous in all his sweaty glory?

Her call to Damien the night before had gone unanswered. Same with the voicemail she'd left, asking him to return her call. He was probably in some far corner of the world where cell phone reception was as crappy or non-existent as it was in the rural areas of Montana.

Still, the man was getting married in two days. The least he could do was call his fiancée each night to whisper sweet nothings in her ear and tell her how much he loved her.

Allie frowned into the mirror at the same time Swede glanced up.

Come to think of it, Damien hadn't said he loved her since the day he'd proposed. Sure, the occasion had been romantic. He'd taken her to one of the most expensive restaurants in Bozeman and then they'd walked along the city streets afterward, arm-in-arm. When they'd come to the city park, the almost-full moon overhead gave just the right amount of light so they didn't need flashlights to see their way.

Damien had stopped, pulled her into his arms and stared into her eyes.

No man had ever held her like that. Most men she knew treated her like one of the guys, until Damien came along and reminded her that she was a woman, with all the needs and emotions most women had.

Then he'd dropped to one knee and asked her to marry him, and she'd been thrilled that a man thought she would make a good wife. But, was that enough to commit her life to a man she still barely knew?

The more she thought about it, the more she realized she might have made a huge mistake by saying yes.

If only she could talk to Damien. Maybe she'd get back that spark of excitement and be happy about the upcoming nuptials instead of feeling like Saturday would be one big disaster.

She was glad she'd insisted on a small wedding with family and a few friends.

The sooner she spoke to Damien, the better. Waiting until the actual wedding would be too late.

In the meantime, Allie drove a few feet forward at a time, gnashing her teeth, counting the bales until they were done. And they wouldn't be done until all of the hay was neatly stored in the barn.

Could this day get any longer?

By late afternoon, the last bale had been stacked in the barn. Though it was late, the sun wouldn't set for another hour or two. The men shook hands and parted, Hank heading home, Eddy heading for the foreman's house for a shower, her father and Swede for the main house.

Allie entered behind the two men and stopped in the kitchen.

Swede stopped, too, turning back toward her.

"Go ahead," she said. "You can have the first shower. I didn't sweat as much as you did." She wandered into the living room, and waited until she heard the water running.

Georgia had run over to the foreman's house for a few minutes, and Allie's father was in his own room showering.

With no one watching her, and her need to talk to Damien so important to her future, Allie decided to make a break for it. Perhaps Damien was back at his ranch and she could corner him for answers to all the burning questions she'd stored up since he left. Number one being, *why the hell did you ask me to marry you?*

She left the house and hurried to the barn. Catching and saddling a horse would take too long, so she pushed the four-wheeler out behind the barn and pressed the start button. The Bear Creek Ranch and the Double Diamond were both large spreads, but they adjoined on the southern border.

Allie had made the ride on horseback several times, and once on the four-wheeler. The terrain wasn't too challenging, and she could get there and back in less than an hour. Surely Damien would be home by now.

She sped away, hoping no one saw her leave. Since her decision wasn't planned, hopefully that attacker wasn't watching. If he had observed her all day, maybe he'd think she was done for the night when she'd gone inside the house. Either way, she was pretty good on the four-wheeler and confident enough in her skills to elude the bad guys. She hoped.

The trip across the ranch took twenty minutes and wouldn't have taken that long if she hadn't had to dismount, open three gates, drive through and close them behind her. Soon she was driving up to the mansion that could be her home in just two days. The broad columns and huge windows were stunning. But, would she fit in that house? Would the place feel like home? Could she be the kind of wife a businessman like Damien needed?

Did she want to be that kind of wife?

The sight of the burned-out hull of the stable and the scent of charred lumber made her want to gag. Nothing had been done to clean up the mess or start building a new stable to house the fine horses Damien kept. Perhaps that would be her first goal as the new wife of the owner. Allie dismounted, climbed the stairs to the front entrance and rang the doorbell.

Miles opened the door. "Miss Patterson, so nice of you to stop by. But I'm afraid Mr. Reynolds hasn't returned from his business trip. Would you care to come in for a cool beverage?"

Not really. Allie needed to talk to Damien.

Miles opened the door wider and Allie entered, wanting to see again what she was getting into by marrying the most eligible bachelor in the county. Hell, maybe in the whole state of Montana. How had she landed a catch like that?

The entryway floors of marble tiles stretched all the way into the main living area at the back of the house with twenty-foot ceilings and windows stretching the full height and length of the room. She could see from the front to the back of the house and through the windows to the snow-capped peaks of the Crazy Mountains.

"Miss Patterson, if you'd like to have a seat, I can get you that drink. What would you like?"

Allie stared around the room, feeling like an inter-loper, a stranger, a square peg in a round hole. This place didn't fit her personality. She'd be afraid to put her feet on the coffee table or wear her boots inside.

"Nothing, Miles. I'm sorry, but I can't stay." Though it never had in the past, the pure ostentatiousness of the decor threatened to overwhelm her now that she stood in the middle of the living room without Damien at her side. She'd mistaken the way he belonged for her belonging there, as well. Now she couldn't get out of there fast enough.

Allie turned and started for the door.

"Miss Patterson, Mr. Reynolds asked me to give you a piece of luggage from the set you two will be taking with you to the Cayman Islands on your honeymoon. Would you like to take it with you now, or would you like me to deliver it to your house tomorrow?"

She didn't want it at all. But she couldn't tell Miles she was getting cold feet. And she didn't want him to make the trip to the ranch, wasting his time if she decided to chicken out at the last minute. "No need to deliver it, Miles," she said.

"Then I'll collect it and bring it out to you in just a moment."

Before Allie could correct Miles and tell him she really didn't want the case, she watched him disappear into the cavernous house.

Great. Now she'd have one more thing to lug back to the ranch, and it would get dusty on the cross-country trip. Feeling like a fool, Allie left the house and walked out to the ATV. From where she'd parked, she stared at the shell of the stable, wondering who would have been heartless enough to destroy such a lovely building, nearly killing the animals inside.

Miles hurried out of the house, carrying a medium-sized, brown leather suitcase. When he noticed she was on the ATV, he stopped and frowned. "I thought you had arrived in your truck. Perhaps I'll deliver this tomorrow, after all."

"No worries, Miles. I can strap it to the back of the

four-wheeler. It won't get any more roughed up than it would be by the baggage handlers at the airport."

"If you're sure." Miles held the case clutched to his chest.

Allie reached for the bag, and Miles handed it over. She strapped it to the rack on the back of the four-wheeler and climbed aboard. "If Mr. Reynolds makes it in tonight, tell him it's imperative that he call me immediately."

"I will," Miles promised. "Stay safe, Miss Patterson."

Allie rode out across the pasture, her heart heavy, the suitcase banging against the rack behind her. The closer it came to her wedding day, the more convinced she became that it wouldn't happen. But, she couldn't call it off without first speaking with Damien. Doing so was only fair. She refused to be a bride who jilted the groom at the altar. A day early was better than when all the guests were seated and waiting.

Halfway back to the ranch, she crested a hill and started down into a valley. So wrapped up in her own miserable decision and the consequences she faced, she didn't hear the other engine over her own until an ATV roared up beside her and rammed into her back tire. Her four-wheeler lurched and swerved toward a drop-off.

Heart thumping, she managed to straighten the steering wheel. She thumbed the throttle, sending her vehicle racing ahead. Fortunately, she was back on the Bear Creek Ranch and she knew every inch of the place like the back of her hand.

Speeding across the rocky terrain, she topped a rise so fast her wheels left the ground for a second and then slammed to the earth on the downward slope. She cursed herself for riding out without carrying the requisite shotgun. Too far from the barn to make it back quickly enough, she had to go in defensive mode. If she could put enough distance between them, she knew of a place she could hide until the attacking rider gave up and went away.

Now would be a good time for her bodyguard to discover her missing and come looking for her.

AFTER ONLY FIVE minutes in the shower, Swede walked out, his towel slung over his shoulders, wearing only blue jeans. He stopped in front of Allie's open bedroom door. Nothing moved inside. He stepped in and looked around. "Allie?" No answer.

Not too worried, Swede entered his bedroom, pulled a clean T-shirt out of his duffle bag and dragged it over his head.

Allie had been downstairs when he'd gone for his shower. He'd let her know it was her turn. Pulling on a pair of boots, he hurried down the stairs, his feet moving faster each step he took, a niggling feeling creeping across his skin. "Allie?"

The back door creaked, and footsteps sounded in the kitchen.

Swede headed that direction only to find Georgia checking the contents of the oven. "Have you seen Allie?" he asked.

Georgia straightened. "I thought she'd gone for her shower."

At that point, Swede's belly clenched. "She's not in her room, nor in the shower. I just came from upstairs."

"What's for supper?" Lloyd entered the kitchen and sniffed. "Something smells good."

"Mr. Patterson, have you seen your daughter since we came inside?" Swede asked.

He shrugged. "Not since I went up for a shower. She might be out at the barn. Although, Eddy said he'd feed the animals. Maybe she decided to help."

"Eddy was in the shower when I left our house," Georgia said. "He didn't say anything about Allie."

"I'll check the barn," Swede said.

"I'll check around the house," Georgia said.

"Why the worry?" Lloyd asked, following Swede out the back door. "She's always fiddling around the barn."

"I just want to make sure she's all right," Swede said.

"Why wouldn't she be?" her father asked.

Swede didn't answer. He opened the barn door and entered. All the horses were in their stalls. Which meant she hadn't taken one out to exercise or ride, she wasn't anywhere around the barn and her truck was in the driveway.

Mr. Patterson stood near the rear of the barn, staring into an empty corner where a four-wheeler had been parked the day Swede and Allie had mucked the stalls. "You don't suppose Allie took the four-wheeler out to check on that sick heifer, do you?"

Damn. Swede walked out the back door of the barn.

As he suspected, he found fresh tire tracks in the dust. Allie had gone out alone on the four-wheeler.

"Sir, do you have another four-wheeler?" Swede asked.

"Nope. Just the one."

"Please, go get Mr. Edwards while I saddle up. We need to find Allie."

"Why are you so worried about her? She does this all the time."

Swede wanted to leave and find Allie, but he owed it to her father to let him know what was going on. "Mr. Patterson, I'm sorry, but we didn't want to worry you. I'm not Allie's friend from college. I was hired by Mr. Reynolds to be her bodyguard. Several attacks have occurred around your daughter. We need to find her before someone else does."

"You mean to tell me that shooter from the other night wasn't just a random act?"

Swede shook his head. "Not only did someone take a shot at us on our way back from the Blue Moose Tavern, he tried to run us off the road. And the day we went out to check on the heifer, a man on an ATV tried to run your daughter over. We need to hurry."

CHAPTER 9

ALLIE ROUNDED A ROCKY CORNER, ducked between boulders, and rode down the middle of a stream for a short distance to hide her tracks and then climbed up the bank into a stand of trees surrounded by low brush. Behind the trees rose a bluff with several caves carved out by centuries of water flowing through the rocks. If she could make it to the caves, she had a chance of hiding inside one she and Hank used to play in as teenagers.

She ditched the ATV behind the brush, jumped off and ran, ducking to avoid low-hanging branches, leaping over medium boulders and glancing over her shoulder every four or five steps.

The sound of an engine nearby made her run faster. She had to make it to the cave before he saw her. The biggest challenge was once she started up the rocky path, she could be visible from below. She clung to the bottom of the bluff for as long as she could until she stood almost directly below the cave entrance. To get there, she had to climb over huge rocks. Eventually, she'd rise above the treetops and scoot along a ledge to enter. A thin waterfall ran out of the mouth of the cave, dropping one hundred feet to a stream. One slip on the climb upward and she could make that same fall and, like the water, splatter all over the river rocks below.

As long as her attacker was still on the ATV, he might not be able to see her climbing up the side of the bluff. He'd have to have a clear line of sight from the bottom of the bluff through the branches of the trees.

Allie took a step, slipped and caught herself before tumbling over the side. Her heart pounded so loudly in her ears she could barely hear anything else. She stopped, crouched low in the rocks, and listened. She could hear nothing but the whoosh of the wind through the trees.

Sweet Jesus. She had to move even faster. If the man had found her ATV, he might figure out she'd gone up the bluff to the caves.

Her muscles ached and her lungs burned with the extra effort to pull herself up the side of the bluff. Finally, she arrived at the cave and fell inside, crawling deeper into the shadows.

She lay still for several minutes, filling her lungs with the cool, damp air, straining to listen for the sound of someone climbing up after her. Allie pushed to her feet, her knees wobbling, her body drained.

Why had she ducked out on Swede? All she had to do was ask him to take her to the Double Diamond Ranch. He would have. If she'd found Damien there,

ELLE JAMES

Allie could have taken him aside, out of earshot of Swede, and told him how she was feeling. Yes, the discussion would have been awkward. But she wouldn't be in the situation she was in now.

The sound of a pebble bouncing off other rocks made her freeze. Allie shrank into the back of the cave near a tunnel that led even deeper. She didn't want to go much farther without a light, but she would, if she had to.

A shadowy silhouette appeared in the mouth of the cave.

Allie swallowed a gasp and slipped deeper into the tunnel.

SWEDE TIED Little Joe to the hitch, ran to the tack room and grabbed the saddle he'd used the last time he'd ridden. Blanket, saddle, girth... he fumbled, trying to remember how Allie had looped the leather strap through the girth. Once he had it tight enough, he ran back to the tack room for the bridle.

"We have to find her, Little Joe," he said to the horse, slipping the bit between his teeth.

Outside the barn, Ruger waited patiently for Swede to give him permission to go with him.

"Come on, Ruger, we have to find Allie."

The dog tipped his head.

Mr. Patterson and Eddy came running from the house.

"We had a call from Miles, Damien Reynold's butler.

He wanted to know if Allie had made it back to the house all right."

"She rode an ATV all the way over to the Double Diamond? It's over five miles."

"By the highway," Mr. Patterson stated. "She probably went cross-country. She knows the way and can get there and back fairly quickly on an ATV."

Then why wasn't she back already? Swede didn't say it, but he could see the same question in Lloyd and Eddy's faces.

"We'll saddle up and be right behind you." Eddy pointed across the pasture. "Head toward the gap between those two hills. You're armed, right?"

Swede patted the handgun beneath his jacket. "I am."

"Good. We'll catch you as soon as we saddle the horses."

Eddy had already disappeared into the barn. Lloyd followed.

Swede nudged the horse's flanks with his heels, and Little Joe sprang forward. God, he wished he'd had the ATV. He wasn't sure he'd be of much use on horseback. Going on foot wasn't an option. He might not reach her in time.

"Come, Ruger!" he called out.

The dog shot ahead of the horse, racing across the pasture like he knew where he was going.

Swede hoped he did. He hadn't trained Ruger to track a person, nor had he given the dog something of Allie's to sniff. But Swede felt more confident with the animal by his side, especially with Little Joe eating up the pasture beneath his feet. Galloping was much easier on the seat than trotting any day, and the gait got him where he needed to go faster. He just hoped when it came time to slow down, the horse would know what to do.

Riding on wings and a prayer, he charged across the pasture, aiming for the gap between the hills. As he topped a rise, the vista changed. On the other side of the hills were more hills, some rocky with steely gray bluffs. This was a different route than Allie had taken him two days before. As he raced through the divide, he hoped Eddy and Lloyd would catch up to him soon before he compounded the problem by getting lost.

Little Joe slowed, the ground beneath his hooves getting rockier and more treacherous. As Swede neared the base of one of the bluffs, he saw movement out of the corner of his eye. At first, he thought it might be a bird flying up the side of the cliff. When he turned and glanced up, he saw a figure in black entering a cave.

Swede pulled back on the reins so hard Little Joe reared and nearly trampled Ruger. Swede held on to the saddle horn and dug his heels into the stirrups, praying the horse didn't tip over backward.

Finally, Little Joe came down on all four hooves.

"Hey!" Swede shouted.

The man in the cave paused and glanced down. He had one hand braced on the wall of the bluff, and he held something in the other hand. Something small and dark...like a handgun.

Swede nudged Little Joe and leaned forward as the horse plowed through brush and trees, crossed a creek and stopped in front of the rocky escarpment.

Even before Little Joe was completely stopped, Swede swung out of the saddle to the ground.

The man at the mouth of the cave turned toward Swede and fired a round.

Swede ducked behind a boulder and waved at Little Joe, afraid the idiot above would hit the horse.

Little Joe spooked and ran, probably headed back to the barn. Ruger crouched next to Swede.

If Swede guessed right, that man up there was after Allie and might have her trapped. He didn't know how deep the cave went. All he knew was the man was armed and had fired on him first. That gave him the right to defend himself, and Allie. However, in order to be effective with a handgun, he had to get closer.

Taking a deep breath, Swede eased out from behind the boulder, spied the next big rock he could use as cover and made a dash toward it, zigzagging as he ran. Ruger ran with him, arriving at the same time as Swede.

Another shot ricocheted off the top of the big rock they ducked behind. Swede performed this maneuver, again and again, moving higher up the side of the bluff, picking his way through the rough terrain as best he could. Within minutes, he was within a reasonable range to fire.

The figure disappeared into the cave.

Damn. Swede took the opportunity to race as fast as he could, stepping over stones, climbing over boulders and pulling himself higher up the trail.

Still, the man didn't appear, making Swede even more anxious, his heart banging against his ribs.

Ruger, on four legs, had much better balance and nimbly climbed the rocky terrain.

"Get 'em, Ruger. Get 'em," Swede said.

The dog raced the remaining yards up the incline and ran into the cave. A shot rang out.

Swede held his breath, praying Allie or Ruger hadn't taken that bullet. Using the remainder of his breath and strength, he heaved himself up over the rocks and ran into the cave.

Though Ruger was only considered a medium-sized dog, he'd tackled and pinned the gunman.

But not for long. The man knocked Ruger to the side, lurched to his feet and dove for his gun.

Swede reached it first, kicking it out the mouth of the cave. The man switched directions and flung himself at Swede.

Barely inside the cave himself, Swede wasn't in a position to take the full force of the man's weight. In a split second, Swede fell to the ground. It was that, or be knocked over the ledge.

The gunman didn't have time to slow his forward momentum. He tripped over Swede's body, stepped in the middle of the waterfall flowing out of the cave's entrance and tumbled over the edge.

He cried out as he plummeted to the base of the falls, landing with a dull thump.

Wasting no time on the dead man, Swede entered the cave, calling out, "Allie? It's me, Swede."

Ruger disappeared into the darkness and whined softly.

"Allie?"

"Swede?" She materialized in front of him, Ruger at her side, his tail wagging a thousand times a minute. For a moment, Allie stared at Swede, her bottom lip trembling.

His heart swelled and he opened his arms.

Allie rushed into them. "I prayed you'd come," she said into his shirt, her voice catching on a sob. "I don't think he would have found me back in the tunnels. But it was really dark, and I've never gone in very deep without a flashlight."

"You're okay, now." Swede smoothed a hand over her hair, speaking to her like he did to the animals in a slow, calming tone, though nothing inside him was calm. He'd almost lost her. She'd been so close to taking a bullet from that man's gun or falling over the ledge to her death on the rocks below.

Swede buried his face in her hair and inhaled the strawberry scent, mixed with the evergreen fragrance of the trees. "You scared the hell out of me."

"I'm sorry." She stared up at him. "I had to go to see Damien."

"I would have taken you."

"I know, but I needed to go by myself."

"And?"

She snorted. "He wasn't there."

Without releasing her, he leaned back enough to cup her cheek. "What was so all-fired important you had to go without me to escort you?"

She stared up at him, her green eyes darkening. "You."

God, he wanted to kiss her. Every beat of his heart

urged him to do it. "Me?"

Allie nodded and reached up to touch his face, her fingers tracing the scar along his cheek. "I can't stop thinking about you."

"Funny," he said. "There must be something in the water." He bent his head, no longer capable of resisting those very tempting lips. Before he took them, he asked, "Are you going to slap me again?"

She chuckled, wrapped her hand around the back of his neck and said, "Not a chance." Then she met his lips with hers, kissing him as long and hard as he kissed her.

Swede slid his hands down her back to the base of her spine and lower, pressing her hips to his. Nothing could stop him from claiming this woman's mouth.

Except the shout echoing off the walls of the bluffs.

"Allie! Swede!" Lloyd Patterson's voice boomed through the gathering dusk.

Swede was first to step away. He stared down into Allie's eyes. "Are you okay?"

Allie nodded, pressing the back of her hand to her mouth. She squared her shoulders and nodded again. "We need to call in the sheriff and an ambulance."

"Or a coroner," Swede said. "I'd be surprised if he survived the fall."

Her jaw tightened and her eyes narrowed. "It's wrong of me to say it, but I hope he's dead."

"Not wrong." He slipped his arm around her waist and eased toward the opening of the cave. "In this case, it was us, or him."

Allie tipped her chin. "I choose us."

"His own actions sent him over the edge. The

landing did the rest." He gripped her hand. "Come on, your father will be beside himself until he sees his darling daughter."

She shot a glance his way. "He knows?"

Swede nodded. "You turned up missing, so I had to tell him. He was well on his way to figuring it out by then."

Allie sighed. "He'll be mad at me."

"Probably," Swede agreed. "But he'll be happy you're alive and well."

"After we get down from here safely." She peered over the edge. "If I remember correctly, it's easier climbing up than going down."

Swede winked. "We'll help each other."

Picking their way over the rocks, they eased their way down the bluff.

Eddy and Lloyd were at the bottom of the waterfall beside the body of Allie's attacker.

"We heard the gunshots and followed the sound," Eddy said.

Lloyd stared hard at Allie.

"I'm sorry, Dad. I didn't want to worry you."

"My ass," he bit out. "Being a target of someone bent on killing you is a no-brainer. You tell me and everyone else around you. That way we're all looking out for you."

Allie pushed her shoulders back. "You're right."

"And don't go running off alone." Her father nodded toward the body on the ground. "He might not be the only one gunning for you. I'm gonna have words with Mr. Reynolds."

"I went over to his place to have a talk with him, myself," Allie said. "He's not in town."

"After what's happened, I want to take a bullwhip to the boy."

Allie touched her father's arm. "Then you'd end up in jail."

Patterson scowled. "It would be worth it. Any man who skips out of town when his fiancée is in trouble deserves to be whipped. Hell, he doesn't deserve the fiancée, and she'd be smart to tell him so."

"Daddy…" Allie glanced around. She nodded toward the body, lying face down on the rocks. "Who is it?"

Eddy stepped across the rocks, checked for a pulse and shook his head. "Didn't think he'd survive that fall." He grabbed the man's arm and turned him over.

Allie gasped. "That's Will Franklin, Damien's foreman." Her brows drew together. "I'll bet he was also the one who blew up the barn."

"The bastard was conveniently in town when it happened," Swede agreed.

"If he wasn't already dead, I'd shoot him myself." Allie glared at the corpse. "That explosion and fire almost killed five horses."

Swede was so relieved Will hadn't succeeded in killing Allie, he almost laughed at her statement. The image of Will with a gun in his hand, so close he could have fired into the cave and hit Allie, stole all the humor out of the situation.

"How did you guys get here?" Allie asked, looking around.

"Horseback," Swede responded.

Allie's brows rose. "You? Out here?"

Swede nodded. "Little Joe did good. But, he's not above leaving me here to head back to the barn."

Turning to her father and Eddy, Allie asked, "And you two?"

"Our horses are tied to a branch near the creek," Eddy answered.

Allie clapped her hands together. "Then let's get back to the ranch."

"Swede, you can ride double with me," Eddy offered.

"Allie can ride with me," her father said.

She shook her head. "I ditched my four-wheeler in the brush. As long as it starts, I can make it back to the barn on my own four wheels."

"And I'm going with you," Swede said.

"Tell you what," Lloyd said. "You three head on back and call the sheriff. I'll stay out here until Eddy brings him out. Don't want the wolves destroying evidence."

Eddy nodded.

Swede followed Allie to the stand of brush where she'd hidden her ATV. It was still there, untouched and undamaged, with that damned suitcase strapped to the back.

Allie climbed on and started the engine. Then she turned to Swede. "Hop on."

He slid his leg over the seat and settled behind her, wrapping his arms around her waist.

Being a bodyguard had its perks, but Swede was sure kissing the fiancée of the man he was working for wasn't supposed to be one of them.

Allie revved the engine and took off. Ruger followed, easily keeping up with the pair on the ATV.

Though he was relieved Will Franklin wouldn't be a threat anymore, Swede wasn't sure Allie was out of the woods yet. What beef could Will have had against Allie? Was he afraid she'd usurp his control of the ranch? Or had someone hired him to carry out the threat that had been painted on the side of the stable?

Swede didn't have the answers and, at that moment, he didn't care. What he did care about was the woman in front of him. The one who smelled like strawberries and evergreen forests. She even had a few twigs sticking out of her wild auburn curls.

God, she was beautiful. The more he was with her, the deeper he fell.

It would be tough delivering her to the wedding and letting go. But, he had to. His job wasn't to steal the bride, it was to protect her and give her to another man in two days.

Pressure threatened to squeeze the air out of Swede's lungs. All those bodyguard rules had flown out the window on his first assignment. He wondered if this was really the job for him in the wilds of Montana, or if he should do something less stressful and go be a deckhand on a charter fishing boat.

A strand of auburn hair floated back on him, brushing across his face, touching him in a way he'd never considered as poignant. It was like a finger stroking him, teasing him urging him to continue to follow this woman, no matter where she led him.

CHAPTER 10

BACK AT THE HOUSE, Georgia met Allie and Swede in the barnyard.

Eddy had beat them back, riding fast and hard to get to a telephone and call 911.

"Oh, thank God!" Georgia wrapped Allie in a bear hug that nearly crushed her bones. "You had us all so worried. I think I lost a couple of years off my life and gained a few more gray hairs."

"I'm sorry," Allie said, her teeth chattering. Darkness had settled in and the night sky, clear of all clouds, had already begun to release the heat of the day.

The older woman clucked her tongue. "Never mind the scoldin'. The important thing is that you're okay." She stared at Allie. "Oh, baby, you're cold. Let's get you inside."

"Really, I'm okay. Nothing but a few scratches and bruises. I could use a hot shower, though." Things for her could have ended a whole lot worse. At least she wasn't dead, like Will Franklin. A twinge of compassion flickered across her consciousness over the man's death, immediately followed by the strengthening of her will. He had tried to kill her on multiple occasions. Swede might have been collateral damage. "I'll be upstairs if anyone needs me."

Allie marched up to her room, gathered clean underwear and a pair of pajamas, a change from her usual oversized T-shirt. Once in the shower, she turned up the heat and stood under the spray until her insides were as warm as her outsides. When she stepped out of the shower to dry off, she started shaking and couldn't seem to stop.

Never had she been more afraid than when she'd been trapped in the cave with a man wielding a gun. That was the stuff Wild West movies were made of. Thinking a cup of hot cocoa would help, she left the bathroom and padded down the stairs to the kitchen.

Through the kitchen window she could see half a dozen vehicles in the barnyard. An ambulance, a couple of sheriff's deputy's vehicles, and a small first-responder fire truck. Allie glanced down at her pajamas. Maybe she should get dressed to speak to the authorities. She debated going back upstairs, but decided she was fully covered and wanted the hot cocoa more.

Once she took the mug out of the microwave, she pulled on a pair of boots and a jacket, grabbed her cocoa and stepped outside.

Half a dozen people surrounded her, all asking questions at once.

Swede worked his way through the small crowd and slipped an arm around her.

Allie leaned against him, grateful for his solid strength and willingness to stand beside her during the questioning. By the time they'd loaded Will Franklin's body into the ambulance and everyone departed, Allie was mentally and physically exhausted.

"Come on, let's get you inside." Swede touched a hand to her lower back and guided her back to the house.

Instead of going directly inside, Allie stopped on the second step up to the porch. "I'm tired, but too wound up to go right to sleep. I think I need to stay out here for a few minutes. The cool night air helps clear my mind. Go. Get your shower. I won't go anywhere." She held up her hand. "I promise."

"I can't leave you outside alone," Swede said.

"Go," a voice said behind him. "Get your shower. I'll sit with my daughter." Her dad walked out onto the porch, carrying a steaming cup of coffee.

"I'll only be a few minutes," Swede said.

"Take your time." Her father lowered himself to the porch step and patted the space beside him.

Allie sat. She couldn't remember a time since her mother died that her father had sat beside her on the porch steps. Tears welled in her eyes, and she fought to keep them from sliding down her cheeks. What was wrong with her? She wasn't usually this emotional.

Since her mother died and Hank joined the Navy, Allie had tried to be everything her father needed, sometimes forgetting what she needed. Which was probably half the reason she'd accepted Damien's proposal of marriage. He'd seen in her a woman. Not a daughter or a rancher. She'd felt special for a brief moment, the typical female with dreams of a fairytale wedding to a handsome man. But she'd been blinded by the wedding planning. Now she had a big mess to clean up, and she was so tired.

Her father reached out and took her hands in his big, callused fingers. "Allie, I don't say it enough, but I love you to the moon and back."

Tears slipped from her eyes and rolled down her cheeks. Once they'd started, she couldn't hold them back. "Oh, Daddy." She leaned into his shoulder. "I've missed you."

"I'm sorry, I haven't been much of a father since your mother died. I miss her so badly some days I don't know if I can go on."

"Me, too."

"She should have been here for you, to talk with you about all the woman things I can't begin to understand."

"You haven't done so badly. And I've had Georgia to lean on."

"What have I taught you, other than how to be an old grouch? Hell, I ran off your brother."

"He wouldn't have made it through SEAL training if not for the way you toughened him up. He told me so himself." She squeezed his hand.

"Tonight, I realized just how close I came to losing you." He looked down at their joined hands. "It scared me. Bad. I don't want to lose any more of my family. I'll fight to keep you safe. So, please, if you're in trouble, let me know."

No matter how independent she was, she still needed her father. "I will, Daddy."

He kissed her forehead like he used to when she was a little girl. "If Damien makes you happy, then I'm all for your wedding. But if he hurts you or you want out, I'll have my shotgun ready."

Allie half-chuckled and half-sobbed. "Thanks, Dad. I'll remember that."

A sound behind them made Allie turn.

Swede stood in the doorway, dressed in clean jeans and a blue chambray shirt, his hair wet, his feet bare.

God, he was the most ruggedly gorgeous man Allie had ever seen.

Her father stood. "I need to hit the sack. We have another load of hay to haul in tomorrow."

"I'll help with that," Allie offered.

"Don't you have to get your nails, hair or some such nonsense done for the wedding?" her father asked.

She smiled. "That happens the day of the wedding." If she went through with it. She needed to talk to Damien. Soon.

Again, her father bent and pressed a kiss to her forehead. "Whatever makes you happy, makes me happy." He entered the house, closing the door behind him.

Swede sat in the spot Allie's father had vacated moments before.

Ruger dropped onto the porch directly behind him and laid his head on his paws.

"Are you okay?" Swede asked.

"I am, now." She wiped the moisture from her cheeks and stared out at the moon, shining high above the Crazy Mountains. "I'm sorry about taking off."

"Yeah. About that..." He leaned his elbows on his knees. "Having a bodyguard necessitates a two-way commitment. I can't do my job if you run away."

"I wasn't running away. I needed to see Damien." She shoved her hand through her wet hair, lifting it off her shoulders. "Alone."

Swede nodded. "And he wasn't there."

She shook her head. "No."

"You could have called ahead and saved a whole lot of trouble."

"I know. I called but no one picked up. And, frankly, I wasn't thinking clearly." *I was thinking of you, you big galoot.*

"Would it help if you got a different bodyguard? Bear and I could switch assignments."

"Is that what you want?" she asked, her voice barely above a whisper. "I know I've been less than cooperative, but I'd rather stick with you...if you don't mind." She plucked at the fabric on the leg of her pajamas.

"Better the devil you know, than the one you don't?" Swede asked.

"No." She glanced up at him, though seeing through the moisture pooling again in her eyes was difficult. "I trust you. I know you really do have my best interests in mind." She leaned into his shoulder. "I promise not to take off without you."

"You won't have to put up with me much longer. The

wedding is the day after tomorrow. Then you'll be on your honeymoon in the Cayman Islands."

Yeah, that was the plan. If she chose to follow it. She reached for Swede's hand. "Thank you for rescuing me in that cave today."

Swede turned, his knees touching Allie's. "I think the real hero today was Ruger."

Allie swiveled toward the dog at the same time as Swede. She let go of Swede's hand and ran her fingers over Ruger's soft fur. "He was amazing. Did you have him specially trained?"

Swede scratched behind Ruger's ear. "He's a rescue from the pound. I picked him up because he was on death row. And to tell the truth, he rescued me."

"How could anyone leave their dog behind when they move on?" Allie shook her head. "How did he rescue you?"

"Since the attack that ended my career in the navy, I've had nightmares. Ruger helps get me through them."

Allie looked up from the dog to his master. "How so?"

"Just by being there. When he senses my distress, he nudges me with his nose. It brings me out of the dream world into the real world. Before Ruger…well, I wasn't coping well."

"He is a hero." She patted the dog's head and pushed to her feet. The more she learned about Swede, the more she wanted to know. With another man's engagement ring on her finger, she had no business learning more about Swede. The personal details only made her see him as a man. An interesting man. One with a love for dogs, which put him way up there on her list of great guys.

No, she needed to see Damien, and end her engagement, or go through with the wedding. Until she did that, she had no right to daydream or night dream about another man.

As she stood, she teetered on the edge of the step and would have fallen if Swede hadn't leaped to his feet, grabbed her arms and pulled her against him.

Allie's hands touched his chest, the hard muscles flexing beneath her fingertips. She had the wild urge to run her hands beneath his shirt and feel the skin stretched over those fabulous muscles.

Jerking away her hands, she got her footing and climbed the remaining steps to the porch. "I'd better go to bed. We have another load of hay to haul tomorrow."

"I'd say stay here and let me handle it, but I need you close, so that I can keep an eye on you. We'll do it the same as last time?"

Allie nodded.

"Allie?" Swede reached for her hand and laced his fingers with hers.

She stared at where their hands entwined, her heart racing, her mouth dry.

"Today scared me more than I've ever been scared in my life." He snorted. "And I've been in some pretty hairy situations." He lifted her hand to his lips and pressed a kiss to her knuckles. "I'm glad you're okay."

Electric currents raced up her arm and down her body to pool low in her belly. This couldn't happen. She couldn't be sexually attracted to a man she'd only known a few days. But she was, and it made her feel more alive than she'd felt...ever. An admission which shook her to the core. Using every bit of control she could muster, she pulled her hand from his, anxious to leave him, before she threw herself into his arms and made a fool of herself.

Swede's hand dropped to Ruger's head. "I'll see you in the morning."

SWEDE WAITED on the porch several minutes after Allie went inside, afraid that if he followed her, he'd stay with her all the way to her bedroom. Once there he'd convince her to make love with him.

Wrong, wrong, wrong!

He stood beside Ruger, the dog nudging his hand, sensing his turmoil.

"Sometimes I wish I were you, Ruger," he said. "Life as a dog is so much less complicated."

The dog whined and licked his hand.

"Yeah. Until you find yourself on death row and a broken-down veteran saves you from the gas chamber." He ruffled Ruger's neck, made a pass around the exterior of the house, looking for anyone lurking, unwilling to presume Will Franklin was the only one stalking Allie. When nothing moved and Ruger didn't snarl or growl in warning, Swede made his way inside to his room on the second floor. Knowing Allie was in the room on the other side of the wall reminded him of how close she was, yet how far she was out of his reach.

He stripped out of his shirt and jeans and lay on the

sheets, naked. The heat he'd felt burning inside when he'd touched her hand and kissed her fingers clung to him, making it difficult to go to sleep. For a long time, he stared up at the ceiling, willing his lust to subside. Time and fatigue finally won the fight, and he fell to sleep.

What could only have been minutes after he'd closed his eyes, Swede was awakened by the sound of quiet sobbing.

Ruger nudged his hand and trotted to the door. Thinking he might have been imaging the noise, Swede listened.

There it was again. The soft sobs were coming from the room on the other side of the wall. He leaped to his feet, dragged on his jeans and hurried out of his room. When he stood in front of Allie's door, he hesitated. If he went in, he wasn't sure he could walk out without touching her. And touching her wasn't all he wanted to do.

Another sob was the deciding factor. He tapped on the door and, careful not to wake her father, called out softly, "Allie."

Continued sobbing made him grab the door handle and twist. It opened easily, and he stepped inside, closed the door behind him and crossed to stand beside her bed before the next sob shook her body.

"Oh, darlin'," he said, his heart clenching inside his chest.

Tears stained her cheeks and her bottom lip trembled. Her legs thrashed, trapped in the sheets. Whatever she dreamed was either breaking her heart or terrifying her. Maybe both.

Swede couldn't stand by and do nothing. He scooted her over on the mattress and slid onto the bed beside her, pulling her into his arms. "Wake up, Allie. You're having a bad dream."

She rolled onto her side, burying her face into his bare chest, her hand resting against his skin.

The strawberry scent of her hair was almost his undoing. He couldn't stay long, or he'd be tempted to kiss her.

She took a shuddering breath, her fingers flexing and curling against him.

Swede tried again, his power of resistance waning with every passing second she lay in his arms. "Sweetheart, you need to wake up. You're dreaming."

"If I'm dreaming, please...don't wake me," she said, her voice low and gravely, spreading over him like melted chocolate.

With a groan, Swede clutched her tighter, his groin tightening, the blood rushing from his brain to parts farther south. He was losing it, and he had no way of letting go.

Allie's hand slid down his chest to his abdomen and lower still to where he'd only half-buttoned his fly.

Swede sucked in a breath, afraid to move lest he encourage her to keep going. This wasn't what he'd come to do. But he couldn't deny the magnetic attraction he had for this woman.

Her fingers slipped beneath the waistband of his jeans.

He covered her hand with his. "Allie, you have to know what you're doing. You can't be asleep on this."

"I'm awake," she said, opening her eyes.

From the little bit of moonlight edging its way through a gap in her closed curtains, he could see her staring up at him. "I should go," Swede said.

Her hand flatted against him. "Please, don't. Stay with me."

"I can't stay and not touch you."

She took his hand and slid it up under her pajama top to the rounded swell of her breast. "Then touch me."

His fingers slowly curled around her breast, weighing the fullness of it in his palm. Swede groaned. "God, you feel amazing."

She reached for the hem of her pajama top and pulled it up over her head, tossing it to the side.

"What about your fiancé?"

"It's over," she said. "I can't marry him."

Swede froze, his thumb and forefinger arrested in pinching her nipple. "Why?"

"After all that's happened, I've learned that I don't love him. I was in love with the idea of getting married, not with the man I was going to marry."

Swede leaned over and kissed the corner of her mouth, then her lips. "But your wedding is in two days," he said against her lips.

"Not anymore. I'm not going through with it," she said. "I'm telling Damien tomorrow."

Knowing he should wait until after she officially called off her engagement, Swede couldn't stop fondling her breast or kissing her lips. What had started as a means to comfort her had become an entirely different scenario he was ill prepared to fight against. This internal battle was one he was all too willing to concede.

The question was, could he live with himself the next day?

CHAPTER 11

THE MOMENT ALLIE felt Swede's arms around her, she knew she couldn't let him go. Her dream had shaken her. She'd been hiding in a dark cave, while a man with a gun stood silhouetted in the light, pointing at her. Her feet had felt cemented to the floor, her heart pounding so hard she couldn't catch her breath.

Then Swede's arms wrapped around her, and more than that, his voice penetrated the dream, bringing her to the surface of consciousness.

Wrapped in his embrace, she turned to him, running her hand across his warm skin, inhaling the light, musky scent that belonged only to him. This was where she wanted to be.

Only she wanted to be closer. Skin to skin. Allie wanted him inside her, filling her, making her complete. What started as a rescue from a dream quickly transformed into an aching need to be with him. A need so strong, she couldn't deny it a moment longer. "Please, stay with me," she repeated.

She laid her hand over his as he fondled her breast, the tingling sensations sending shocks of electricity throughout her body. At a touch of his lips, she opened to him, thrusting her tongue between his teeth, meeting him halfway in a long, sensuous caress. Allie pulled her top over her head, desperate to be with him, to feel him against her, their hearts beating together.

Swede's lips brushed across hers, kissing a path down the side of her neck, stopping long enough to tongue the wildly beating pulse at the base of her throat. As he moved downward, he nipped her collarbone, kissed the top of her breast and sucked a nipple into his mouth, pulling gently, tapping the nipple with the tip of his tongue until it hardened into a tight little bead.

Allie arched off the mattress, wanting him to take more.

He obliged, drawing more of her into his mouth, flicking the tip, again and again.

Taking momentary control, Allie guided him to her other breast. "Please," she moaned softly.

And he did please, nibbling the peak, rolling it around on his tongue and laving it until Allie thought she would come apart.

Swede moved his lips across her ribs, past her belly button and onward to the elastic waistband of her pajamas. Inching the fabric down her legs, he paused to kiss the tuft of hair over her sex. Then again to lick the inside of her thighs, and finally to nip her ankle as he tossed the garment to the floor.

Allie parted her legs automatically, making room for him to slide between.

Swede lifted her knees, positioning them beside his head and then slipped his finger through her curls. He parted her folds, touched his tongue to that little strip of flesh packed with what felt like thousands of nerve endings, sizzling with heat, sending messages to her brain and back to her core, making Allie slick with desire.

Just when she thought it couldn't get better, he pressed a finger to her entrance and swirled.

"Oh, God," she said, digging her heels into the sheets, pushing her hips upward. "Oh, God."

He pushed two fingers into her and licked her nubbin in a long, slow stroke, pushing Allie to the very edge of sanity.

She teetered on the brink until he flicked and teased her there, thrusting his fingers in and out at the same time. The combination rocketed her to the heavens, flinging her past the stars. She held onto his hair, riding the wave all the way, her core pulsing, her breath lodged in her lungs until she finally drifted back to earth and sucked in a lungful of air. Then need drove her to tug on his hair, drawing him up her body.

He leaned over her, pressing his lips to hers for a brief second.

"You're overdressed," she commented.

"I'm working on it." Swede rolled off the bed onto his feet and shucked his jeans, retrieving his wallet from his pocket as he did.

He was beautiful in a purely male way, with shoulders impossibly broad, narrowing to a trim waist. Firm, six-pack abs and...yes...his shaft jutted out straight and proud.

Allie's channel convulsed, liquid sliding through, dripping onto the sheet. "Hurry," she said, her belly tight, her lungs dragging in air in spasms.

"Protection." He pulled a foil packet from his wallet.

Allie leaned up, snatched it from his hand and applied it, rolling her fingers down his length. She fell back against the mattress. "Oh, sweet Jesus. Please. I can't wait another minute."

"Beautiful, and impatient." He spread her legs, running his hand up the insides of her thighs to the apex where heat radiated. Swede pulled her bottom to the edge of the bed, hooked her legs over his arms and pressed his cock to her entrance.

"Now," she urged. "Take me now."

He thrust into her, driving all the way to the hilt before he stopped. Her channel was so slick with juices inspired by all the foreplay, he slid right in, filling and stretching her deliciously.

Allie grabbed his ass and held him there, letting her body adjust to his length and girth. Then she eased him away and back in again.

Swede took over from there, moving in and out, gradually accelerating until he pumped in and out like a piston on an engine.

Raising her hips to match his every thrust, Allie urged him on, the friction causing the heat to build.

Swede's face tensed, his jaw tightened, and he threw back his head. If they'd been alone in the house,

Allie was sure he'd have shouted or called out her name.

Instead, he slammed into her one last time and remained buried deep within, his cock pulsing, his muscles tight, his face set. Then he scooted her back on the bed, crawled up beside her and pulled her into his arms.

Allie nuzzled his chest, finding a little brown nipple. She touched it with her tongue, loving the taste of this man. Pressing closer, she basked in the skin-to-skin contact, her heartbeat slowing, her breathing returning to normal. Gone were the residual effects of the nightmare. In its place was the utterly poignant satisfaction of great lovemaking with an amazing man.

As she drifted to sleep, a nagging twinge of guilt made her stomach churn. Tomorrow, she'd break off her engagement. Tomorrow, she'd call off the wedding. Even if nothing came of her relationship with Swede, Allie knew in her heart, she didn't love Damien. A marriage between them would never have worked.

She wished he had been home earlier that evening so she could have made the break then. Tomorrow would have to be soon enough.

SWEDE LAY FOR A LONG TIME, loving the feel of Allie in his arms, her soft body pressed up against his hard one, the smell of strawberries wafting beneath his nose. This must be what heaven felt like. He couldn't imagine anywhere else being as wonderful.

But the longer he lay there holding the woman he

found himself falling for, the more that kernel of guilt grew into a sour wad in his gut. He'd made love to his client's fiancée two nights before their wedding. Not only had he broken the first rule of being a bodyguard, he'd betrayed Hank's trust and risked the reputation of the company his friend was trying to build. With Hank's sister.

Allie slept, seemingly dream-free.

After a while, Swede slipped from the bed, disposed of the condom, pulled on his jeans and left her room, closing the door behind him. From now until Allie called off the wedding, Swede vowed to keep his hands to himself. Touching Allie was strictly forbidden.

He returned to his room and lay on top of the covers, his hand reaching for Ruger's head and the calming influence of a dog who didn't judge. For a long time, he stared up at the ceiling, counting the minutes before sleep finally claimed him again.

MORNING CAME TOO SOON, the sound of Mr. Patterson clomping down the hallway in his cowboy boots waking Swede without need for an alarm. Groggy and with a slight headache pressing against his temples, Swede rose from the bed, dressed, brushed his hair and teeth and went downstairs to the kitchen.

"Eddy and Mr. Patterson already had breakfast." Georgia plunked two plates full of food on the table. "They're gearing up, and said for you and Allie to join them when you're ready."

Allie appeared, her hair pulled back in a ponytail,

her face scrubbed clean. No makeup masked the simple beauty of her complexion and eye color.

Her cheeks were naturally blushed and her gaze didn't actually meet his.

"Did you sleep all right?" she asked.

"Yes," he answered. "And you?"

She nodded and took her seat across the table.

They spent the rest of the meal eating, not talking, the atmosphere strained. For such an amazingly close connection the night before, he felt like they were miles apart that morning, even though he could reach across the table and touch her face.

Having only pecked at her food, Allie got up, took her plate to Georgia and gave her a wry smile. "Guess I'm not very hungry. Could you save that for my lunch?"

"Sure can." Georgia's brows dipped. "Are you feelin' okay?"

Allie nodded. "Just a little tired."

"Maybe you should stay in and let me do the driving today."

"I think the fresh air will do me good." Allie kissed Georgia's cheek. "But thanks."

Swede carried his half-eaten plate of food to Georgia. "Thanks for breakfast. You're a great cook." He, too, kissed Georgia's cheek and winked. "See you later."

Georgia touched her cheek, her gaze following Allie out the door. "Look out for my girl out there."

"I will." Swede wouldn't let her out of his sight for a minute. He refused to allow anything to happen to her. His heart was riding on it.

The day flew by in a rush to get all the hay from the

second pasture baled, loaded onto the trailer and unloaded into the barn.

Allie drove, not saying much to anyone. Not that the men were in the mood to talk. All of their energy was channeled into the work. By the time the sun crept toward the horizon, Eddy tucked the last bale onto the top of the stack in the barn. "Done."

"What say we have a beer to celebrate?" Lloyd draped a sweaty arm over his daughter's shoulders.

"Thanks, Dad, but I'll pass." Allie lifted her father's arm off her shoulders. "And you smell."

"Good, honest sweat."

For the first time since Swede had met Mr. Patterson, he saw the older man grin.

"That's right, you have a wedding to get ready for." His eyes narrowed. "Aren't you supposed to go out on the town for a bachelorette party or something?"

"No, Dad."

"Why not?"

"I don't feel like it." She turned toward the house.

"What about a rehearsal?"

"Damien and I opted not to do a rehearsal." She gave a weak smile. "I'm headed for the shower."

Swede hesitated before following her.

"Go on," Mr. Patterson said. "Eddy and I will take care of the animals."

"Thank you, sir." Swede hurried after her.

She was up the stairs and in the shower before he caught up.

If he expected any acknowledgement for the best night of sex he'd ever had, he wasn't getting any. He wondered if she really was going to break it off with Damien. Swede's gut tightened. If not, he'd been played for a fool.

But the more he thought about it and everything he'd seen of Allie, she wasn't the kind of woman to play games. That woman was a straight shooter. The more likely reason for her silence today was that breaking her engagement was heavy on her mind. Because she was a straight shooter, she was probably feeling a crap load of guilt for having slept with her bodyguard.

At least that's what Swede hoped.

CHAPTER 12

ALLIE SHOWERED the dust and itchy hay off her skin, telling herself she'd feel better making the call she had to make with a clean body, if not a clean conscience. After she'd toweled dry, she dressed in shorts and a T-shirt and crossed the hallway. Her gaze drifted to Swede's bedroom, part of her hoping he'd open the door and give her an encouraging smile. She'd need all the encouragement she could get to make that call.

With no one stopping her to engage in conversation, Allie entered her room like she was walking to her doom. Taking a deep breath, she squared her shoulders, lifted the phone and dialed Damien's cell phone number, fully expecting to get the voicemail.

He answered on the second ring. "Alyssa, dear. I'm so glad you called."

"I thought you would be back by now," she said, startled into saying the first thing that came out of her mouth.

ELLE JAMES

"I'm sorry, sweetheart. Business delayed me. I'll be back tomorrow morning."

"The wedding is scheduled for tomorrow, or had you forgotten?" she said, with a little snap in her voice.

"I know. I can't wait for the ceremony that will make you Mrs. Damien Reynolds. Then we leave immediately for our honeymoon."

"About the wedding—" she started, then had to swallow.

"Don't worry, darling. I'll be there on time. Until then, sweet dreams."

"But, Damien—"

The connection ended.

What the hell?

She dialed his number again and the connection went straight to his voicemail. She hung up and redialed, repeating the process four times until she finally gave up. Mad as hell and ready to end their engagement, she was tempted to do it by voicemail. But she couldn't. No matter how aggravating the man was, he deserved to be told to his face that she wouldn't marry him.

She stared at the clock on the nightstand. As late as it was, she wouldn't have time to contact everyone to tell them not to come to the wedding. What she'd tried so hard to avoid would come to pass. She'd jilt her groom at the wedding.

She stretched out on her bed, fully expecting to lie awake all night long, dreading the next day's confrontation with Damien. And she did. For a while, going back and forth on whether she'd marry him just to save face, and then have the marriage annulled a week later. Of course, she wouldn't go on the honeymoon. But Damien could at least enjoy the time on the beach. The Cayman Islands had been his idea of the perfect honeymoon. Not hers.

Allie would rather have gone to a mountain cabin where they could be alone, making love into the wee hours of every morning. Now, she couldn't picture making love to Damien at all. In her heart, it was Swede. And she couldn't go to him that night because, though she'd gone against her own code of honor and slept with him the night before, she couldn't do it again until she'd made a clean break from Damien.

So she lay in bed, irritated that she couldn't talk to Damien, and so sexually frustrated she thought she might explode.

Finally, she fell to sleep and woke the next day with dark circles under her eyes and a splitting headache. Which fell in line with the expected wedding day from hell.

SWEDE TOSSED and turned all night long, getting up several times with the full intention of marching into Allie's room and kissing her until she was completely convinced Damien Reynolds was not the man she should marry. Each time, he talked himself out of doing it. Swede was afraid she'd change her mind and marry the bastard anyway.

Allie needed to come to a decision on her own. She said she was going to call it off, but she hadn't come to him to let him know the deed was done.

By morning, Swede assumed it wasn't. Which meant his final duty as a bodyguard was to get Allie to the church on time that morning. He scraped the stubble from his chin, combed his hair, and dressed in pressed black trousers and a white button-down shirt. Strapping on his shoulder holster, he tucked his nine millimeter pistol in place and shrugged into his black suit jacket. Like it or not, he was going to a wedding.

In his best boots, he walked down the stairs, hating that he was taking the only girl he'd ever considered worth the trouble of settling down with to marry another man. He'd talk to Hank and hand over the job of protecting his sister to him. He lifted the phone on the table in the hallway and dialed Hank's number.

"Hello," a female voice answered.

"This is Swede; I'd like to speak to Hank."

"Hi, Swede. This is Sadie. How's Allie holding up?"

"Okay. I guess. She's still in bed as far as I know."

Sadie laughed. "She'd better get moving if she's going to make it to the church on time. Oh, wait. Here's Hank."

"Swede, Bear just walked in the door. Sadie and I are heading to the church as soon as he's debriefed me. I'll see you there." Hank hung up before Swede could ask him to take over his bodyguard assignment. Swede would have to deliver her to the church after all. *Great.*

Footsteps on the staircase made him glance up as he set the phone in the cradle.

Allie descended, wearing her usual jeans and a T-shirt, her hair pulled back in a simple ponytail. She carried a long white garment bag and a pair of white satin shoes. Dark circles beneath her eyes stood out against her pale face.

"Hey," Swede said, reaching for the bag. "Let me."

She held it against her chest, refusing to hand it over. "I can carry it." Allie glanced around him. "Have you seen the others?"

As if on cue, Georgia appeared in the kitchen door. "I've made some muffins you can eat on the way to the church."

"I'm not hungry, but thank you," Allie said.

"You can't get married on an empty stomach," Georgia said. She held up a brown lunch sack. "I packed them for you. You better get going, or Sadie and I won't have time to do your hair. Eddy, your father and I are following you in my van. I have decorations loaded in the back. Eddy's going to help put them on the pews. We'll see you in a few minutes." Georgia disappeared back into the kitchen.

Swede glanced down at Allie. "Ready to go?" He'd wanted to say anything but that. But Allie looked like she had a lot on her mind, and he couldn't make himself bring up the subject of the elephant in the room. Was she going through with the wedding, or would she call it off at the last minute? Swede prepared himself for the former, praying for the latter.

ALLIE LED the way out to her truck. "I'll drive," she stated, climbing into the driver's seat.

On the thirty-minute drive into Bozeman, hardly a word was spoken between them. Swede studied the road ahead and behind, looking out for any signs of trouble. His gut told him Will Franklin wasn't the only one involved in the threat against Allie. And until they found out who was behind it all, he wouldn't consider her safe.

Allie parked in the church parking lot and carried her dress inside. Once through the door, she turned to the right and entered an anteroom where Sadie was waiting with a smile and an assortment of brushes and curling irons. "There you are," she exclaimed excitedly. "Let's get you ready for a wedding."

Swede made a sweep of the room, checking all doors and where they led. He made sure they were locked and secure. "I'll be in the vestibule. If you need me, yell." Swede left the room, not waiting for an answer.

Georgia sailed past him, carrying a veil. "See you fellows in a few minutes."

Swede went in search of Hank, his heart heavy. Hank wasn't in the vestibule so Swede entered the sanctuary.

"There you are." Hank approached him, his face tense. "I have news from Bear."

"Shoot."

"Three more soldiers from that same unit have been attacked since they'd gotten home. All of them were more or less gutted. Those three weren't as fortunate as Baker. They died before anyone could get to them."

Swede swallowed the bile rising up his throat. Three men who'd served their country, killed at home. "Anything stand out other than that they were in the same unit?" he asked.

"Bear talked to the commander and found out the four soldiers had been invited to a party on the last night of their deployment. They came back so intoxicated, they couldn't remember anything about the party the next day."

"Intoxicated? In Afghanistan?" Swede shook his head. "I didn't think they were allowed to bring booze into the country."

"They weren't, but the contractor who threw the party must have smuggled in some. My guess is, that because they couldn't remember anything from the night before, they were slipped some kind of date rape drug."

"Why?"

"Why would they all be cut open when they returned to the States?"

A horrible thought came to Swede, making his belly churn. "They were being used as God damned mules to smuggle something out of the country."

"Bear dropped by the Medical Examiner who processed one of the men. He didn't find any traces of drugs around the incisions or in the intestines."

"Where did Baker say their unit was stationed?"

"He didn't. But Bear found out from the company commander that they were on the edge of the Badakhshan Province."

"Isn't that province known for the lapis lazuli gemstone mining?" Swede asked, glancing around to make sure they weren't overheard.

Hank's eyes widened. "It is. And for the rampant smuggling of gemstones out of the country."

Swede closed his eyes, anger burning in his gut. "Who was the contractor?"

Hank's face grew taut. "RM Enterprises."

"Aren't they the contracting company that won the majority of the bids to rebuild or construct much of the Afghan infrastructure?"

Hank's lips pressed into a thin line. "Guess who one of the partners in that company is?"

Swede's heart slipped into his belly. "Damien Reynolds, the R in RM?"

"You got it," Hank confirmed. "His partner is a Frenchman by the name of Jean-Claude Martine. From what Bear found out, Martine has a wicked temper. Afghanis who crossed him had been rumored to disappear."

Swede headed for the door. "We need to tell Allie. ASAP. Where's Bear now?"

Hank followed. "He's contacting the FBI, the local police and anyone else he can get on short notice. This place will be lit up like the Fourth of July when everyone gets here."

"In the meantime, we need to keep Damien from making a run for it," Swede said.

"Right. Bear will also have them on the lookout for Martine."

Swede exited the sanctuary and entered the ante-room where Georgia and Sadie were helping Allie prepare for the ceremony.

Georgia was tucking a strand of hair into an updo on Sadie's head when the men barged in.

"Where's Allie?" Swede asked.

Sadie smiled. "She excused herself to go to the bathroom one last time before she put on her dress."

"How long ago?" Hank demanded.

"Not more than five minutes." Sadie's brows furrowed. "Why?"

His pulse racing, Swede responded, "She might be in trouble."

ALLIE KNOCKED on the door of the room the groom should be dressing in.

"Yeah," came the answer.

Still dressed in her jeans, her hair hanging down around her shoulders and no makeup on her face, Allie entered, dread churning her belly.

Damien stood in the middle of the room in front of a long mirror.

Miles stood behind him, brushing his hand over the crisp white shirt, smoothing away imaginary wrinkles.

Allie's gaze swept from the top of his neatly combed dark hair to the tips of his shiny black, patent leather shoes. Damien Reynolds turned heads no matter where he went. Why he'd asked Allie to marry him was beyond reason.

Damien glanced her way. "Darling, I'm not supposed to see the bride before the ceremony."

Allie smiled at Miles. "Could we have a moment?"

Miles nodded and left the room.

"What's wrong?" Damien took her hands and stared down at her clothes, his brows dropping into a frown. "You're not even ready."

"Damien, I can't marry you."

"What? Nonsense. Of course you can. You're just getting cold feet. It happens. Once the ceremony is over, you can relax on our way to the islands." His hands tightened on hers. "You did bring the case I had Miles give you?"

"It's on the back seat of my truck, but I'm serious." She pulled her hands out of his and reached for her engagement ring. "This week, I had time to think about us and I…I'm sorry, Damien." Now that the initial declaration was made, she felt only relief. Allie slid off the ring and tried to give it to him. "I don't love you. I don't think I ever did. I was more in love with the idea of getting married than being married to you."

He held up his hands, refusing to take the ring. "You can't back out on me now. We're getting married in a few minutes."

"I am backing out." She set the ring on a nearby table and moved a few steps away. "I tried to tell you last night, but you hung up on me. I tried calling you all week, but you didn't answer. I would rather have told you all of this before our wedding day. I'm sorry it had to be this way. But our marriage wouldn't have worked."

Damien's face changed from shock to anger. "You can't leave. We're getting married. Go get into your dress."

Allie shook her head and turned to leave.

Damien grabbed her arm in a painful grip and yanked her around. "Look, you can't jilt me. We have to get to the Cayman Islands today. Do you hear me? We're getting married, and that's the end of it."

Throwing up her hand like she'd learned in self-defense class, Allie knocked Damien's grip loose. "Don't touch me ever again. You don't need me to go to the Cayman Islands. Go without me. Goodbye, Damien. Oh, and I hope you figure out who destroyed your barn." Allie stepped out of his reach and hurried for the door.

"Damn you, Allie!" he yelled and made another grab for her.

She'd done what she'd come to do. Allie ran out of the room and down the hallway to the exit. Now that she'd called off her engagement to Damien, whoever was threatening him would have no need to torment her. Footsteps pounded on the tile floor behind her. She glanced over her shoulder at Damien chasing after her.

Allie burst through the side door of the church leading to the playground. She ran around to the front where she'd parked her truck. She could have gone back inside and asked her father or Eddy to drive her home, but right now, she couldn't face them. And Damien was going all whacko on her. She dove into the driver's seat and shut the door just in time.

Damien body-slammed into the side of the truck and slid to the pavement.

For a moment, Allie thought he'd hit his head and hurt himself. She opened the door and got out, stepping over his body.

"Damien?" She bent to shake his shoulder. That's when she saw a bright red stain on the back of his shirt, spreading wider with each second.

As her brain registered that it was blood, she heard a

sharp popping sound followed by the window behind her shattering. *Damn.* Someone was shooting at her. Allie threw herself to the ground beside Damien's inert body, glancing all around for the source of the gunshots.

A man ran toward her, his gun held out in front of him.

Allie rolled beneath the truck and out the other side. Before she could get her feet beneath her, someone grabbed her by her hair and slammed her head into the side panel of her pickup.

The blue sky of Montana went black.

CHAPTER 13

SWEDE RAN toward the room Damien was supposed to be dressing in for the wedding. He was met in the hallway by Miles, Damien's butler.

"They're gone," the older man said, his face paler than usual.

"Who's gone?" Swede demanded.

"Mr. Reynolds and his fiancée." He pointed to the exit at the end of the hallway. "They ran out that door."

Swede pushed past the man and sprinted for the exit. Outside, he found himself near a playground. A scream sent him running toward the front of the building, Hank close on his heels.

A man in black trousers lay face down on the ground next to Allie's truck, blood staining his white shirt.

"Allie!" Swede shouted, drawing his Glock from the holster beneath his jacket.

"Swede! Be careful! He's got a gun!" she shouted from the other side of the vehicle.

A man who looked like the picture Hank had shown him of Jean-Claude Martine stood, dragging Allie by her hair, a gun with a sound suppressor pointed at her head. "Move, and I'll kill her."

"I'm not moving." Swede held up his empty hand. "Just don't hurt the girl."

"Where's the damned suitcase?" the man said, pulling back hard on Allie's hair. "I want that damned suitcase."

Her face was red, her neck extended back. "What suitcase?" she breathed.

"The one Reynolds gave you. I want it now." He pressed the gun into her temple.

Swede glance around, searching for a miracle to get Allie out of the situation. "Martine, let her go. You're not going to get very far."

"Shut up!" He fired into the air and then put the gun to Allie's head again.

"The police and the FBI are on their way. They know you and Reynolds are behind the killings of the soldiers."

"They won't take me. Not as long as I have her." He turned Allie so that her body was positioned in front of him. Again, he spoke next to Allie's ear. "Where is it?"

"In the truck," she said, gasping. "Take it. I didn't want it in the first place. I intended to give it back."

"It wasn't Reynolds's to give in the first place. I made all the sacrifices. Reynolds didn't have the stomach for it, once we started."

"Let go of the woman," Swede said. "Take the suit-case and the truck. Just leave the woman."

"No way. She's my ticket out of here. I'm going, but I'm taking her with me. Make any moves toward us, and I'll kill her. Just try me." He opened the passenger side of the vehicle and tried to shove her inside.

"Swede, don't worry. He's nothing but a rattlesnake." Allie started to climb in, stumbling, her head tipped back so far she probably couldn't see. Then she fell, slipping down to the ground, bringing Martine's hand down.

Swede had only one chance. He had to make it count. He raised his weapon and squeezed the trigger before Martine could jerk Allie back in front of him. The bullet left the chamber.

For a long moment, Martine stood there, his eyes widening. The gun he held to Allie's head slipped from his fingers and dropped to the ground, discharging a round. Then he slumped like a rag doll slipping from a child's hands. His body landed on top of Allie.

Swede ran toward them. "Allie!" Fear knifed through him. Had the bullet from Martine's gun hit Allie?

He rounded the hood of the truck, grabbed Martine's arm and dragged him away from Allie.

She lay still for a heart-stopping moment, her eyes closed, a bruise on her forehead rising into a goose-egg-sized lump. Then she blinked her eyes open and stared up at Swede. "Is he dead?" she whispered.

A huge wave of relieve brought Swede to his knees. "Oh, sweet Jesus, Allie. Yes. He's dead."

Hank rounded the truck and stared down at his

sister. "Oh, thank God, she's all right. The cops and the fire department are here. I'll bring them over." Hank left them alone, hurrying over to the emergency vehicles gathering in the church parking lot.

Allie smiled and raised a hand to her forehead, touched the bump and then winced. "That's going to leave a mark."

Swede laughed, gathered her into his arms and held her for a long time, his heart so full he thought it might explode. Allie was alive, the bad guys were dead and all was right with the world, again. His eyes stung with tears, and he blinked them away.

She reached up and cupped his face, her finger tracing the scar on his cheek. "Are you okay?"

He choked on a laugh, his throat constricting. "I'm okay."

"Thanks for killing that rattlesnake."

"You're welcome."

"And for the record, I'm glad you're my bodyguard."

He swallowed against the constriction in his throat. "I am too. You've got a pretty darned amazing body to guard."

She held up her ring finger. "I broke off our engagement before…before that man shot Damien. I'm a single woman."

"That's a good thing, because I'm planning to ask you out on a date."

"What's stopping you?"

"Not a damned thing." He bent to press his lips to hers in a tender kiss. "Allie Patterson, would you go out with a washed-up old navy guy?"

She tilted her head, pausing for a long moment.

Swede held his breath, searching her sweet face until she finally responded.

"No."

His heart skipped several beats and he frowned. "No?"

"No." Her brows dipped low. "But I would consider going out with a highly skilled bodyguard who can shoot like nobody's business." Her smile flashed. "I figure I'll never have to worry about rattlesnakes again."

Swede laughed and hugged her to him.

She pushed away enough to look him in the eye. "I have one condition."

"What's that?"

"Ruger comes along with us."

"Deal."

Then he kissed her, believing for the first time he might just have found his place in the civilian world, on a path to that happy ending he never thought could happen to him. If he played his cards right with Allie, he might be heading in that direction, starting with their first date.

Two weeks later

Swede leaned against the stone fireplace at the White Oak Ranch, a long-neck beer in one hand. He studied the group of men gathered in Hank's house.

Besides himself and Bear, a SEAL from their old unit had joined their ranks, along with another soldier from

D-Force who'd worked with them on one of their joint operations back on active duty.

Hank stood in the middle of the room, never more in his element since he'd left the navy. "Brotherhood Protectors is growing fast. Apparently, there's more of a need for personal security services than I'd originally anticipated, and word is spreading fast. I'd like to welcome you aboard and thank you for giving this organization a chance."

Bear shook his head. "No, Hank, thank you. We're just glad to have jobs."

Hank dipped his head. "You all come highly recommended, and have special training and weapons skills."

"Yeah. For what it's worth." Former D-Force soldier, Carson 'Tex' Wainright rocked back on the heels of his cowboy boots.

Ben 'Big Bird' Sjodin, sat in a leather armchair, his long legs stretched out in front of him. "We're highly trained in combat skills, but there aren't too many opportunities as a civilian to use that training."

"Exactly," Hank agreed. "The challenge is to remember our clients aren't all familiar with the military way of thinking. We need to be open to learning about our clients' lives and what it will take to keep them safe."

Swede chuckled, thinking of Allie and how she'd taught him a few things about ranching. He was getting better at horseback riding and caring for livestock. And he'd taught Allie a few things about shooting she didn't already know. That had been their second date.

"The assignments can be more dangerous than we

originally expected," Hank said. "So, don't let your guard down." He nodded toward Swede. "Swede's first assignment was protecting my sister Allie from some seemingly unexplainable attacks. We found out her fiancé was involved in smuggling gemstones from Afghanistan to the U.S., using soldiers as mules. Five people died in that operation. Three American soldiers, Allie's fiancé and his partner."

"His point is, don't think this will be a cakewalk," Swede said.

Hank picked up a handful of file folders. "The good news is we have work. Plenty of it." He glanced in the folders and handed them over to each man, one at a time. "Look over your clients' portfolios and requests. If you have questions, ask now."

The men studied their folders and compared notes, asking various questions about locations and protocol.

After the formal part of the meeting was over, Sadie joined Hank, her hand on her belly, which had begun to show a bit of a baby bump.

"Anyone need another beer?" Allie entered the room, carrying five long-necks. She made her way around the room, dropping them with the men, and coming to a stop in front of Swede. "Who'd you get?" she asked, leaning over his shoulder.

"An older woman afraid her neighbor is planning on taking over the country," he said, liking that she was interested.

Allie's eyes narrowed. "Older woman?"

Swede shrugged. "Really old. Thirty-six."

She crossed her arms over her chest. "I'm not so sure

I like the idea of you being a bodyguard to another woman. How do I know you won't fall in love with her?"

"Jealous?" Swede pulled her into his arms and brushed his lips across hers.

"Maybe." She lifted her chin. "You're growing on me, and I don't want to lose you to a cougar."

"We've been out together on fourteen dates, one for each day of the week since we started dating. You're not losing me to a cougar, bobcat or any other kind of feline." He nuzzled her neck. "I have my own little Allie cat. Sweetheart, I'm in this for the duration."

She wrapped her arms around his neck and kissed him back. "Good thing, or I'd have to hire you as my permanent, personal bodyguard."

Swede kissed her long and hard, convinced he'd found the woman for him. Two weeks wasn't a long time, but he knew in his heart he wouldn't find another woman like her. "Babe, I'll guard your body any time you want. How about now?"

Allie threaded her hand in his, glanced around at the others in the room, and, with a wink, tipped her head toward the door. "I'll show you where the teenagers go to neck."

"A woman after my own heart." He chuckled and followed her out of the house. She hadn't been after his heart, but she sure as hell had it in her capable hands.

Enjoy other Military books by Elle James

Brotherhood Protectors Series
Montana SEAL (#1)

Bride Protector SEAL (#2)

Montana D-Force (#3)

Cowboy D-Force (#4)

Montana Ranger (#5)

Montana Dog Soldier (#6)

Montana SEAL Daddy (#7)

Montana Ranger's Wedding Vow (#8)

Montana Rescue

Take No Prisoners Series
SEAL's Honor (#1)

SEAL's Ultimate Challenge (#1.5)

SEAL'S Desire (#2)

SEAL's Embrace (#3)

SEAL's Obsession (#4)

SEAL's Proposal (#5)

SEAL's Seduction (#6)

SEAL'S Defiance (#7)

SEAL's Deception (#8)

SEAL's Deliverance (#9)

Visit ellejames.com for more titles and release dates
For hot cowboys, visit her alter ego Myla Jackson at
mylajackson.com
and join Elle James and Myla Jackson's Newsletter at
Newsletter

MONTANA D-FORCE

BROTHERHOOD PROTECTORS SERIES
BOOK #3

New York Times & USA Today
Bestselling Author

ELLE JAMES

New York Times & USA Today Bestselling Author

ELLE JAMES

MONTANA
D-FORCE

BROTHERHOOD PROTECTORS

CHAPTER 1

MIA CHASTAIN TWISTED the key in the lock and pushed open the door to her past. Eleven years had passed since she'd been back, for more than a night or two, to the house in which she'd been raised. After she'd left for college, she'd sworn she'd never return to Eagle Rock, Montana. Except for very short visits, and her parents' funeral, she'd kept that promise to herself. Yet, here she was. Entering the house her great-grandfather had built, with the intent to stay for at least a month.

"Are you sure you want to stay here tonight?" Sadie McClain, her old friend from high school stood behind her, carrying the smallest of the suitcases Mia had packed for the trip home. "It's been a year since anyone has been inside this house. It probably needs a good cleaning before you can sleep here."

"I'll be all right. I can cover a lot of ground in the cleaning department in the hours before bedtime."

"I can stay and help, if you like," Sadie offered.

185

Mia paused with her hand on the doorknob. "You have a husband to go home to. I'll be fine. Besides, I came to Montana for a break from the traffic and noise of city life. I need the chance to regroup and refill my creative well before I start writing my script."

"What you're telling me is that you want to be alone, and I need to scram as soon as I set down this suitcase." Sadie raised her hand. "Don't deny it. I understand your motives. After living in L.A., I needed the peace and quiet of the Crazy Mountains, too."

"Yeah, and I need the time to myself to go through the old place."

"It's been quite a year, hasn't it?" Sadie set the case on the wooden porch and hugged her friend. "I miss your folks, too."

After her parents had passed away the summer before, Mia hadn't had the heart to come home and face the ghosts that lingered in the shadows of Eagle Rock.

Sadie's gaze swept the front of the house. "Don't pay any attention to Marly's comment about this place being haunted. She's just a kid. They enjoy making up stories about deserted places." Sadie rubbed the gentle swell of her belly. She'd just begun to show at five months pregnant. "But if you do get scared, don't hesitate to jump in your car and come stay at the house with us. We have loads of room."

Mia's lips quirked upward at what the waitress at the café had said about her old home. The young people around town thought the house was haunted. It had sat for an entire year without anyone in it, but they swore they saw lights shining through the windows at night.

"Ghosts in the house are the least of my worries," Mia muttered. "I have a deadline. That scares me more than any old ghost."

Sadie smiled. "That's the spirit." She covered her mouth with her hand. "Oops. No pun intended."

The old clapboard home had been Mia's one safe haven in the small town she'd lived in all her young life.

Now that her parents were gone, she needed to decide what to do with the house. Should she sell it, tear it down, or rent it out? To sell or rent it, she definitely had to do some major cleaning and possibly remodeling. At the very least, it needed some repairs. But those would all have to wait.

Deciding what to do with her parents' place was only part of the reason for her being in Eagle Rock. The main focus of her stay was to work through her writer's block on the script due to her editor in less than a month. Under contract to produce, she didn't have time for a gap in creativity. She had to charge forward and get it done. Or buy back her contract and tell the studio that had optioned the work that she had changed her mind about writing the story after all.

The problem was that the story was too close to home for her. Mia could kick herself for proposing it in the first place. Though it would be a work of fiction, it would drag up so many old, disturbing memories she wasn't sure she could handle it.

Every time she sat down to write, her hands shook so much she couldn't keep them rooted on the keyboard of her laptop. Images flooded her mind and filled her with the terror she'd experienced that day thirteen years ago.

The day she'd been raped walking home from the school bus stop.

A chilling sense of being watched brushed down Mia's spine. She spun to look behind her, but no one was there.

"What?" Sadie glanced around. "Spider walk over your grave?"

Mia shrugged and forced a smile to her lips. "No. I'm just tired from the trip." She stepped into the old house, waited for Sadie to cross the threshold, and then closed the door behind them.

Sadie wandered into the living room. "I remember doing homework with you on that rug." Her lips lifted in a sad smile. "It's too bad you don't live here full time. I could imagine our children growing up in Eagle Rock, going to the same school and coming over to each of our houses to do homework. They'd have sleepovers, go horseback riding and generally raise hell." She laughed softly. "Maybe someday?"

With a noncommittal shrug, Mia said, "Maybe." No child of hers would grow up in Eagle Rock. Not as long as the man who'd attacked her remained free and anonymous.

Mia's gaze went to Sadie's belly.

God, she'd never considered that others might be in danger by her not coming forward and reporting her rape to the police.

Sweet Lord, what if Sadie's baby was a girl? What if she was attacked on her way home from school?

Mia bit down hard on her lip. She hadn't told anyone about what had happened to her. Not even her best friend, Sadie, or even her parents. She'd carried the burden alone, feeling dirty and ashamed, as if she'd brought the attack on herself.

As an adult, she knew how foolish those thoughts were. But as a sixteen-year-old, she couldn't have faced her peers if they'd known she'd been used, her body sullied. For weeks she'd lain in bed, afraid she would end up pregnant with her attacker's baby. He hadn't used protection. Hell, he hadn't expected her to live.

Sadie's hand on her arm brought her back to the present. "What's wrong, Mia?"

Shaking herself out of her morose memories, she forced a smile to her face. "Nothing. It's just sad to see the house this way. Mom always tried to make it cheerful and full of light."

"All you need is to open the curtains and windows to let in sunlight and fresh air." She yanked back a curtain, stirring up a cloud of dust. Sadie coughed. "Okay, well maybe you should slide them back slowly." She waved her hand in front of her face. "Mia, come stay with us until this place is livable again."

Mia shook her head. "Thanks, Sadie, but I've needed to do this for a long time. The only way to get it done fast is to live in the disaster zone." She wiped a finger across an end table, leaving a long streak in the thick layer of dust.

Sadie nodded. "Okay, have it your way. But at least let me walk through the house with you once to make sure nothing is glaringly wrong. Then I'll leave you to it."

"Deal."

Mia and Sadie walked through every room on the first floor, and then on to the second floor. No one hid in the closets or under the beds.

By the time they'd been through the house, Mia felt a little better about staying there alone.

She walked Sadie to her SUV and hugged her. "Thank you for welcoming me home."

"I wish you'd let me do more."

"Maybe tomorrow you can come for a cup of tea?"

"I would love that." Sadie hugged her again. "I've missed you."

"I can't imagine you've had much time to miss me with that big, handsome SEAL keeping you busy." Mia grinned. "I always thought you and Hank belonged together. I'm surprised it took you this long to figure it out."

Sadie's face glowed with her love for the man. "We had to be in the same place at the same time for it all to come together."

"Thank goodness he came home when he did, or you might not be here now." Mia squeezed Sadie's hand. "It's great to see you, again."

"I'm so glad you're here," Sadie said. "I get lonely for female companionship."

"You have Hank's sister, Allie."

Sadie nodded. "When she's not ranching. But you speak the language of the movie industry. It's nice to share stories. I'm just happy." She climbed into the SUV.

"See you tomorrow. But remember, if you get scared tonight, come on over."

Mia was already scared, but she'd have to get used to it. "Thanks."

Once Sadie left, Mia entered the house, closed the door and locked it behind her.

Then she faced her past.

She'd left everything as her parents had the day they'd gone to Bozeman for doctors' appointments a year ago.

Their appointments had been in the morning. Apparently, on their way back, they'd been caught in a freak blizzard, had run off the road and rolled down a steep embankment. If they hadn't died in the crash, they would have died of exposure. She could only hope their deaths had been instant and painless.

They'd lain at the bottom of the hill upside down in her father's old pickup, the snow covering their tracks, and eventually, the truck. No one had known to look for them until Mia had called the next day.

They hadn't answered. Having heard about the blizzard in Montana, Mia had been worried. She'd called all the people she knew in Eagle Rock and couldn't find her parents. After a couple of hours, she'd notified the sheriff's department.

The sheriff himself had gone to their house to check on them. No one had answered his knock. Concerned for their safety, he'd broken the lock and entered. He'd found a note on the calendar Mia's mother kept on the refrigerator. The note had indicated they'd had doctors' appointments in Bozeman the day before.

After the sheriff had verified with the doctors' office that the couple had been there the day before, he'd sent his deputy out on the highway to Bozeman to look for any signs of the Chastains' truck.

Mia sighed. The dustcovers over the furniture made the living room appear filled with the ghosts the people in town believed haunted her old home. And really, weren't there? The ghosts were the memories the furniture conjured. Fleeting images of her parents sitting in their favorite recliners, staring at the fire or watching television.

They'd been older when they'd had Mia. She was the baby they'd tried for years to have, and when they'd finally given up in their forties, she'd surprised them.

She couldn't have asked for more loving and giving parents. They'd been a bit old-fashioned compared to some of the younger parents, but that had been part of their charm.

Pushing back the memories, Mia continued through to the kitchen. She'd left all the utilities on throughout the year to keep pipes from freezing. Other than a layer of dust, she could move right in and do what she'd come to do.

She ran her finger along the counter, leaving a clean streak amid the dirt that had gathered since her mother's death. Standing around staring at the dirt wasn't going to get the place cleaned.

If she planned to live there for the next month, she had to get to work cleaning. Once that was done, she hoped to settle, free of distractions from the internet, and write the script she'd contracted to finish before the end of the month.

Rolling up her sleeves, she pulled back her hair and secured it in a ponytail, and then got out a bucket, rags and soap and went to work.

By nightfall, the kitchen sparkled, and she had the kettle on the stove for tea. She'd also cleaned her old bedroom, replacing the musty sheets with a fresh set she'd brought with her from her apartment in Los Angeles.

At the very least, she could have supper and a place to sleep for the night. Tomorrow, she'd work on the rest of the house. When she had it cleaned, she'd start working on her manuscript.

The hard work had kept her from dwelling too much on the past. Exhausted from the trip and all the work, Mia showered, dressed in her favorite, worn T-shirt and soft jersey shorts and then settled at the kitchen table to drink a cup of tea and eat the crackers and cheese she'd brought with her from L.A.

Night had settled around the house. All of the windows had blinds or curtains she could close to block out the darkness, except in the kitchen. The window over the sink stared at her like a dark specter, making her skin crawl the longer she looked at it. She'd have to go to Bozeman to find a set of blinds to cover it.

During the day, the more windows she could open to let in light, the better, but at night, the darkness frightened her. Yeah, she'd learned to get around, even at night, but it didn't stop the irrational fear of being watched from threatening to overwhelm her.

Mia rose from the table, having eaten very little, dumped her tea down the drain and rinsed her cup. All the while, she refused to stare out the darkened window that overlooked the back garden.

When she turned away to go to her bedroom, she could swear she saw a shadowy figure in the window, just out of the corner of her eye.

She grabbed a butcher knife from the drawer and turned to face the window. The view was just as black as it had been when she'd been drinking her tea.

For a long time, she stared at the window, waiting for that ghostly shadow to reappear. Had she imagined the figure? Were her fears getting the better of her?

After a few minutes, she relaxed and started to replace the butcher knife in the kitchen drawer. On second thought, she carried it with her to her bedroom and laid it on her nightstand.

The shadow could have been a result of her memories and her overactive imagination, but she wasn't taking any chances.

She had a gun, but it was packed away in her suitcase that she had yet to unpack. Perhaps that would be the first thing she dug out in the morning. If she continued to feel insecure through the night, she'd unpack it sooner.

Mia slid between the sheets and pulled the blanket up to her chin. Leaving the lamp shining on the nightstand, she closed her eyes and tried to sleep.

Tired beyond endurance, sleep came despite the debilitating fear, only to be filled with nightmares, her memory regurgitated from long ago.

She'd just gotten off the school bus, on her way home from school. Her house was only a half of a mile out of Eagle Rock, surrounded by hills and ranch land. Her great-grandfather had settled in Montana, homesteaded a six-hundred-acre spread and raised cattle and horses. Since then, the successive generations had sold off portions of the old homestead until all that remained was the original house and ten acres.

Mia swung her backpack over her shoulder and started down the driveway leading to her house, set back from the road, past a stand of trees.

Thinking of the homework she had yet to complete, and going over conversations she'd had with her friends during the day, she wasn't aware she was being followed, until a man wearing a black ski mask leaped from the brush and grabbed her from behind.

At five feet two inches, she hadn't been big or strong enough to defend herself. He'd thrown a bag over her head, tied her wrists together behind her, dragged her into his truck and driven her out to a deserted road in the surrounding hills.

Terrified, she'd strained against her bindings, breathing in her own hot, damp air, tears soaking the burlap.

When the truck came to a stop, her attacker had tied her to a tree and pulled off her clothes. She'd fought, kicked and screamed. No one came to save her when he'd penetrated her, tearing through her virginal wall. He'd pinched, bitten and tormented her for what felt like hours, and then left her there to die in the cold air of an early, Montana spring night.

A loud crash yanked her from the nightmare to fully awake. Mia sat up in bed and looked around. At first she didn't recognize where she was, until she spotted the photograph of her and her parents smiling by the lake that summer before her childhood had ended.

She tried to remember why she'd woken. A sound. Something crashing.

Mia reached for the phone on her nightstand, only to remember she didn't have one. Instead, she grabbed the butcher knife she'd left there earlier and swung her feet to the floor. Her heart thumping hard against her ribs, she poked her head out the door of her bedroom. Nothing moved. Darkness enveloped her. Making a mental note to buy nightlights at the hardware store, she inched her way down the hallway to the top of the staircase and shined her flashlight to the floor below.

Another sound captured her attention, this time above her. It sounded like the soft skittering of leaves blowing across concrete. A shiver slid across her skin.

The sounds above had nothing to do with the crash that had jerked her out of her nightmare.

Mia descended the stairs, slowly, wishing she had her gun. Another mental note: dig the gun out of her suitcase.

At the bottom of the stairs, she felt a cool breeze against her bare legs. The air conditioner hadn't kicked in and she hadn't left any windows open.

Another couple of steps placed her near the front entry and the doorway to the kitchen.

The cool breeze was stronger here, coming from the kitchen.

Mia turned abruptly and flashed her light into the kitchen.

A black shadow scurried across the floor and through the open back door.

Mia screamed and backed away, bumped into the wall and dropped the butcher knife. It fell within an inch of her bare, big toe.

Her heart thundered in her chest, and her breath lodged in her throat. Grabbing her purse from the hall table, Mia jammed her feet into her cowboy boots and ran out the front door.

In seconds, she was on the road to Sadie's house, terror fueling her to press the accelerator to the floor.

She had locked the back door before she'd gone to bed, and the black cat that had wandered in sure as hell hadn't broken open the door, damaging the doorframe in the process.

MONTANA D-FORCE (#3)

ABOUT THE AUTHOR

ELLE JAMES also writing as MYLA JACKSON is a *New York Times* and *USA Today* Bestselling author of books including cowboys, intrigues and paranormal adventures that keep her readers on the edges of their seats. With over eighty works in a variety of sub-genres and lengths she has published with Harlequin, Samhain, Ellora's Cave, Kensington, Cleis Press, and Avon. When she's not at her computer, she's traveling, snow skiing, boating, or riding her ATV, dreaming up new stories. Learn more about Elle James at www.ellejames.com

Website | Facebook | Twitter | GoodReads | Newsletter | BookBub | Amazon

Or visit her alter ego Myla Jackson at mylajackson.com
Website | Facebook | Twitter | Newsletter

Follow Me!
www.ellejames.com
ellejames@ellejames.com

ALSO BY ELLE JAMES

Voodoo on the Bayou (#1)

Voodoo for Two (#2)

Deja Voodoo (#3)

Cajun Magic Mysteries Books 1-3

Billionaire Online Dating Service

The Billionaire Husband Test (#1)

The Billionaire Cinderella Test (#2)

The Billionaire Bride Test (#3) TBD

The Billionaire Matchmaker Test (#4) TBD

SEAL Of My Own

Navy SEAL Survival

Navy SEAL Captive

Navy SEAL To Die For

Navy SEAL Six Pack

Devil's Shroud Series

Deadly Reckoning (#1)

Deadly Engagement (#2)

Deadly Liaisons (#3)

Deadly Allure (#4)

Deadly Obsession (#5)

Deadly Fall (#6)

Covert Cowboys Inc Series

Triggered (#1)

Taking Aim (#2)

Bodyguard Under Fire (#3)

Cowboy Resurrected (#4)

Smokin' Hot Firemen

Love on the Rocks

Protecting the Colton Bride

Heir to Murder

Secret Service Rescue

High Octane Heroes

Haunted

Engaged with the Boss

Cowboy Brigade

Time Raiders: The Whisper

Bundle of Trouble

Killer Body

Operation XOXO

An Unexpected Clue

Baby Bling

Under Suspicion, With Child

Texas-Size Secrets

Cowboy Sanctuary

Lakota Baby

Dakota Meltdown

Beneath the Texas Moon

Made in the USA
Monee, IL
23 October 2023

45048394R00118